THE IDIOT KING

Ghostspeaker Chronicles Book 3

PATTY JANSEN

Capricornica Publications

GET FREE EBOOKS

CHAPTER 1

THE LETTER was written in cramped, barely literate hand. The writer had used cheap paper which turned pen strokes into blobs and did not improve its legibility. Neither did the poor light that fell into the boat shed through the open front.

Fleuris LaFontaine had given the letter to Johanna only after she had specifically requested to see it, twice, and Master Deim had asked him to give it to her and Fleuris could no longer go on ignoring Johanna's presence. He had pushed it across the rough wood of the simple table with his be-ringed, delicate hand, wrists barely protruding from the lace cuffs—*dirty* lace cuffs to be sure. Nothing in the refugee camps was still pristine.

Johanna had taken the letter, coolly, chin in the air, and said, "Thank you." She'd unfolded the sheet, making sure that the men in the room wouldn't notice that her hands trembled. Those men continued their discussion, as if she weren't there, about the occupation of Saardam, and people who had or hadn't made it out and assets that may or may not have been destroyed.

Most of it was pure speculation, but they spoke as if those statements were fact.

Johanna had just calmed down from being angry about being told that the Council of Nobles meeting was for *men of import* and not for *wives or consorts*, and now she got angry again. This was how stupid rumours started in the camp of refugee Saarlanders, because the nobles speculated idly, and then the other people took their words for fact, *Because they were important men*. Because people had been waiting for news for weeks and the waiting and endless days of no news were getting on everybody's nerves.

"What does it say?" Roald, who sat next to her, leaned over her shoulder to read.

She smoothed out the letter.

In loopy writing, it said at the top,

To the Red Baron of Gelre and all he deems notifiable in matters of the city of Saardam.

The date at the top said 14th June, which was barely a week after the fateful day that Saardam had burned. Apparently this letter had been delivered to the castle in Florisheim over two months ago, so evidently the Baron didn't consider the former citizens of Saardam immediately notifiable. And that in itself said something about what the Baron really thought of the survivors.

I hereby notify the barony that as of today, I have taken up the position of Governor of the city of Saardam on behalf of the Belaman Church and its rightful supporters. All heathens, disbelievers, disciples of treacherous beliefs and followers of dark witchcraft have been purged from the city. Most of the other citizens have been spared and have in fact welcomed our move. No commerce or ships were harmed. We will do our utmost best to resume the river trade as soon as possible.

Your friend,
Alexandre Trebuchet

"What does he mean—no commerce was harmed?" Roald asked, his too-loud voice cutting into the genteel talk of men that was going on around them.

They stopped talking, most of them looking annoyed.

Johan Delacoeur pursed his lips. He stroked his moustache. "He means that no shops or other businesses were harmed in Saardam, Your Majesty." He dipped his head, but his voice had a tone as if he were speaking to a small child.

"Everything he writes is a lie," Roald said. "A lot of businesses were burned. All along the harbourfront. I saw it."

Fleuris LaFontaine had been drumming his fingers on the table and now thudded his flat palm on the tabletop. "He means that no stock was harmed."

"It's still a lie. The whole city was on fire."

"Shh, Roald." Johanna put her hand on his arm. After weeks of begging, the Council of Nobles, who effectively ran the refugee camp, had finally run out of reasons not to allow Roald to attend. The begging had been Johanna's, under the encouragement of Master Deim, who sat at the far end of the table and who smiled at her every now and then but had been mostly silent during the meeting.

Roald, though, was unaware of the intricacies of the situation. "The whole city was on fire. I saw it. My parents are dead. Everyone is dead!" His voice rose to a squeal.

"Shhh, I know. Calm down." She spoke softly, but was acutely aware of the penetrating gazes of the rich and influential men of the council, those who had been King Nicholaos' advisers and those who, along with the rest of the kingdom, had been unaware of the condition that inflicted his son.

Roald jammed his hands between his knees and sat stiff as a board. The continual tensing and relaxing of his muscles told Johanna that he would probably start swaying soon, or that he'd bang his head into the wall if he got close enough to one.

Master Deim said, "Your Majesty, we are sure that a lot of people in Saardam, most of them in fact, are still alive—"

"But I have never seen any proof," Johanna said. In fact, the only proof she'd seen pointed in the opposite direction. Stories from people in the camp about raiding bandits killing everyone who got in their way or setting fire to houses with entire families inside.

"Everyone is dead! There was blood everywhere and fire everywhere."

"Roald, please, calm down." She put an arm over his shoulder, if only to stop him swaying.

His distress brought back memories of their flight, of the chaos in the palace where she had lost Father, of the buildings on fire in the harbour, of the munitions depot being blown sky-high. Of the dead king and queen, and she hadn't even told Roald that she had seen their bodies. Maybe he had seen them, too. He had never spoken of what happened to him that night and how he came to be in the water in the harbour by himself.

Ignatius Hemeldinck rolled his eyes. He was easily the youngest of the nobles, with his pale hair tied back in a ponytail at the nape of his neck. "Seriously, do we need to hold these important meetings in the presence of an idiot? It's hard enough taking difficult decisions on our own."

"This idiot is your king," Johanna said, primly.

Or Roald would be their king once the coronation ceremony had been held. But that had been put off until the time that the King's sceptre and crown could be retrieved from the cleaning cupboard where Johanna had hidden them. If that cupboard, in fact, still existed.

And the council wasn't making any decisions and hadn't made any for about two months. All that happened in these meetings, according to Master Deim, was that they speculated and pontificated about what had happened and said little about how to go forward.

Ignatius said, "It's not necessary for him to be here. King Nicholaos would allow us to deal with day-to-day issues." He seemed to be making a point of not looking at Johanna.

If that's the case, then it's no wonder that King Nicholaos got into trouble. "The occupation of Saardam is not a day-to-day issue."

"King Nicholaos would also never have allowed interfering women to our meetings."

"I am your Queen according to the law. I accompany my husband."

Ignatius' mouth twitched.

Johan Delacoeur gave his colleague a wary look that seemed to say *shut up while you're still ahead.* He was the oldest of the nobles, grey-haired, thin, wary and suspicious. An old army commander who Johanna didn't particularly like, but had come to respect.

Ignatius took the unspoken advice, leaning back in his chair while heaving a sigh. He wasn't going to repeat what, according to rumours, he'd said the other day about Johanna's marriage to the prince. Not in the presence of the few powerful supporters Johanna had in the camp: Master Deim; the mayor of Saardam, Joris DeCamp; and Captain Arense of the Nielands' ship *Prosperity,* which had brought most of the nobles to Florisheim. The Shepherd Carolus, a young man by the name of Dirk Goedthart, who had been training under Shepherd Romulus, was also meant to be there, but according to Fleuris LaFontaine, he was always late *doing some bleeding-heart thing for the children or something.*

The secretary was busily scribbling in the corner, noting down what people said. He sat against the wall of the boat shed, which was made from clay-daubed wood, with the big notebook on his lap.

"Let's keep talking about this letter," Johanna said. "Like why the Baron has taken so long to show it to us, and what we should do now."

"We have already drafted a response," Johan said, and the secretary in the corner nodded. "Will you read it to the meeting?"

The man leafed through his papers, until he found what he was looking for with an "Ah, here it is. It says: Esteemed colleague—"

Johanna said, "He's not esteemed. He's head of an occupying army."

The man eyed her sideways and continued reading, "Esteemed colleague, thank you for your correspondence—"

"—Thank you for invading our city and burning it to the ground."

"Please, can you let the man read?" Fleuris sounded annoyed.

Johanna crossed her arms over her chest.

The secretary lifted the paper so that he couldn't see Johanna. "Thank you for your correspondence. In light of the recent events, we would like to send a delegation to negotiate the return of authority of the city to us. We would be most delighted if you could meet with us—"

"I was thinking we should say something like: stop killing our families. You're nothing more than a bandit. Get out of our city before we chase you out, and, if you resist, string up your heads over the city gates."

Roald clapped his hands. "Yes, yes, yes. It's our city."

Fleuris rolled his eyes. "That is plain bluff and he will know it. We are too few to amount to much of an army."

"We are, together, the richest people of Saardam and the entire low country. Surely we can hire an army?"

Johan Delacoeur scoffed. "Fight a battle for your homeland with a mercenary army? Who has ever heard of such folly!"

"King Ivan of Bresnia had no problem with it."

He snorted. "What do you know about armies and fighting? A woman, young enough to be my daughter." But his attempt at derision did not hide the impact made by her knowing of the Battle of Dravik, and of how a young king had bought his troops' loyalty. *Thank you, Father, for forcing me to read all those boring history books.*

"Fighting is not how we like to do business," Fleuris said. And doing business, of course, was all that mattered.

"Do you have any business with this man Alexandre?"

He scoffed. "Of course not." In a *what-do-you-think* kind of way. "But he seems to have gotten the marauding savages under control."

"I was under the impression that he *brought* the marauding savages. He invaded. He used fire magicians to burn down much of the city, and then he took possession of it. So, in the light of those things, the king is not going to sign a letter addressed to Alexandre Trebuchet that has the word *esteemed* in it."

Fleuris went red in the face, but before he could say anything, there was the sound of running footsteps outside, and a moment later a man in a brown robe came into the shed: Shepherd Carolus. His cheeks were red, his blond hair stood in all directions, he had smudges on his cheeks and his habit was covered in straw. He sat down at the far end of the table next to Joris DeCamp, panting. "My excuses. I didn't know you'd started already. We bought some straw. I wanted it inside before it started raining again." He wiped his face. The golden chain with the symbol of the Triune dangled around his neck.

His sheer bulk dwarfed poor Joris DeCamp, who was a very slight man. The Shepherd's hands were huge, with thick fingers covered in freckles and hair—very dusty hair to be sure. He was like a normal man, but one-and-a-half times the size, who never shied away from helping people with his sheer strength.

Johanna smiled at him.

The interruption had leached the redness from Fleuris LaFontaine's face. He continued in a milder tone, "Let the correspondence be handled by men who are well-versed in conversing with people of Alexandre Trebuchet's standing. He is a direct cousin of the Burovian king."

"Are you afraid of him?"

"Alexandre Trebuchet has many connections."

In other words: *yes*. And the nobles probably had some business connections tied up with him.

"Whatever letter we write is not going to change our immediate situation here. We need to do *something*. People in the camp are suffering because they don't know what has happened to their families. We have been here for months and we've heard nothing. Winter is coming and most of them are sleeping in tents. I'm sure most of us would like to return."

"We don't know that it's safe to do so. The Red Baron has assured us that he's in discussion with Alexandre, and he's sent messengers to Saardam."

"The Baron's men? Why should they care about *our* city?" She gestured at the letter. "It's really simple: I want this man, this Alexandre, this fire magician, gone. I want to rebuild. I want to know if the people who didn't make it out of the city"—*Father*—"are safe. I want to go back before winter comes."

Fleuris snorted in his *Dumb woman* tone. "You don't understand anything about the situation."

"All right, then. I've given you my thoughts. What do you

think we should do?" *Sit here and eat the Baron's food while we wait until he tells us what he wants from us in return?*

"Well . . ." Fleuris placed the fingertips of both hands together. His many gold rings glittered in the light that fell in through the open door of the boat shed. His fingers were pudgy and looked like sausages. He was in his middle years, with a face that had lost none of its pudgy roundness in the camp. His cheeks were full and made him look younger than he really was, and made his eyes look piggy. "We have been in contact with the Baron and have it from his authority, and that of the leaders of the Belaman Church, that they are restoring order in the city."

"The Belaman Church does not rule Saardam," Shepherd Carolus said, and he wiped his face again. His cheeks were still red.

"He's right. What business does the Belaman Church have in Saardam? And if the Baron has sent people to Saardam, why haven't we heard any news? Why haven't we heard anything from any of our families and contacts?" Seriously, what was wrong with these men? Why were they happy with other people sorting out the trouble? "Are you happy with the Belaman Church taking charge of our city?"

"Of course not."

"Then why aren't you angry that we've been waiting here for months while the Baron has had this letter for all this time?"

"Young lady, you are presuming far too much. The Baron probably only received it recently. He is our friend—"

"I am your queen and you will address me as such."

Fleuris gave her a hard stare. He didn't say anything, but his expression held a *We-will-see-about-that* warning. "The Baron has his reasons which he has already revealed to us, his trusted friends." He breathed in through flaring nostrils.

"Contrary to your assertions, the Baron is helping us a great deal."

"The Baron has lent us tents and given us items of furniture. I'm grateful for that. But what other help is he giving us? He hasn't visited the camp for weeks. I've seen him once since we arrived, and he never even spoke to Roald. Has anyone spoken to him recently? Have there been any signs that he has even sent people to Saardam to talk to this Alexandre? And on the off-chance that I missed their departure—which would be hard to do, since we're camped right next to the river—but on the off-chance, why hasn't he come here to ask for our representatives? Why, for that matter, should *he* negotiate on our behalf?"

"Because he knows Alexandre Trebuchet much better than any of us."

"Isn't that a reason to keep an eye on both of them?" She spread her hands, frustrated.

Fleuris said, "You can't possibly understand. This is a thing between men of certain standing and influence."

And so the bottom line was that, besides being female, Johanna didn't meet the criteria of "standing", and hadn't earned the trust of the circle of nobles that stretched across borders and involved many royal families and their wide and entangled family trees. Alexandre Trebuchet, Roald had informed her, had been a fellow guest at the work farm for difficult royal sons where Roald had spent most of the past few years and which seemed to be the source of much of the trouble.

Johanna said, holding her back straight, "I think the time that we rely on others to do things for us has passed. Baron Uti may mean well, but his concern is his own land. We will make our own investigations. We will write back to this Alexandre." Her eyes met those of the secretary. "We will let him know that his occupation of Saardam displeases us greatly and we will return to resume our rightful position. We will use stronger words that still carry your approval."

She met hard stares around the table. "Or does anyone here actually like that a foreigner sits in our palace?"

"Of course not," Fleuris LaFontaine scoffed, but he sounded less than genuine.

"Then I will see to it that it is done." She rose. She would have the letter delivered by two volunteers who would go to Saardam and report on the situation there. Men from the camp, not the Baron's men.

Roald was staring at the boat shed's dark ceiling and appeared to have been counting ceiling beams, probably to stop himself sliding into a screaming fit. "Come." Johanna pulled him up gently by his arm. Then she looked at the ceiling again. The undersides of the ceiling beams were exposed. If the singing in her blood was anything to go by, they were made of willow wood. She had an idea.

"Her Majesty the Queen declares the meeting finished," Ignatius Hemeldinck said, his voice sarcastic.

"I'm glad that someone here recognises my status," she said, equally sarcastic. She strode past him out of the shed.

CHAPTER 2

"**M**Y CHILD, you're playing with fire," Master Deim said when the meeting had finished. They were slowly walking back from the boathouse along the riverbank.

A bit further along the curve of the Rede River, the *Lady Sara* and the *Prosperity* lay moored at the jetty that would normally be used by the river ships that came to pick up milk. The cows normally grazed in the paddock that had now become a jumble of mismatched tents. It was almost midday and trails of smoke rose from cooking fires between those tents.

The path along the riverbank was quite narrow, so Master Deim walked first, turning around when he spoke. Johanna had hooked her arm through Roald's. He was distracted by some animal in the reeds and she held him so that he didn't trip. His tenseness had abated a bit and he no longer shook or swayed.

"Would you have let them talk over your head as if you didn't exist?" Johanna asked Master Deim. "I don't know what's going on, but those men have done nothing for us. The people are getting unhappy. They want to know when we're going back, or, if we're not, what the reason is, but we've heard nothing and they're doing nothing. Why do they think that the Baron can sort it all out for us? Do they know something we don't?"

"Yes, they probably do. There are many gentlemen's agreements between noble families. They're not going to divulge those agreements to others, not even to their peers." Master Deim shook his head. "They have only barely allowed you to be present. Do you really think it's a good idea to turn them against you already?"

"They were never going to be helpful."

Roald said, "I heard them talking. They were laughing about me. They called me The Idiot King."

"They did indeed. It's disgraceful."

"I'm not an idiot." He pronounced the word *idiot* slowly as if allowing it extra time to sink in.

Johanna shook her head. Whatever you wanted to call Roald, an idiot he was not. With his simple way of looking at relationships, he often understood matters well enough, even if he was clumsy at voicing those thoughts. "Those men are insufferably rude. They're far too used to getting their way. If they were merchants, they would have not a customer left."

"But they are not merchants. They are dangerous men from the most connected, most experienced noble families."

"And that's the reason I have to be grateful to them that they let me come to a meeting where we should have been invited in the first place? I have to be grateful for every word they say? They've always been against us. They have no respect, not for their wives, their fellows or their king. I don't think they ever did." She suspected they had played games with King Nicholaos, and the king, stricken by grief over the death of his daughter, had not seen it.

This was what Father had been talking about when she

was with him in the coach underway to the ball. This was why the King's envoy had asked Father, and not the nobles, for a loan.

Master Deim said, "Yes, they were probably happy with Nicholaos as figurehead king, as long as he didn't get into their way. They were born into power. They like their power and will do whatever they can to hold onto as much of it as they can."

"But then why haven't they done anything about the occupation? Why do they just accept whatever scraps the Baron throws them?"

He spread his hands. "There are many possible reasons. Because they are comfortable doing what they're doing? Because they don't like to risk themselves and their wealth in fighting conflicts they're not sure they can win. Because they hope to be given a position at the Baron's court? Some of them are distantly related to the Baron and other nobles in Florisheim."

"I don't think I'll ever understand that world." She had been exposed to it a little bit through her mother, a minor royal of the Aroden court. When Mother was still alive, Countess Josafina, Mother's great-aunt, would sometimes visit her house. Johanna would have to dress up and sit on the stiff couch in the formal sitting room, while the Countess gossiped about who said what and who was marrying whom, while Mother looked on and occasionally smiled at Johanna or brushed her hair to the side or reminded her to sit still.

"They expect patronage. If you look after your peers, they will look after you."

Of course she knew about patronage, of the arts, usually. The Burovian king had been a patron of Rinius for most of his life. But the habit of noble families to send their unruly and entitled sons to other noble families in order to get them straightened out was not one she understood.

Master Deim added, "Also, child, don't forget that most of them are afraid of magic. This Alexandre appears to have rather a lot of it, and is not afraid to unleash its full force onto the common people. Saardam has always been so poor in magic that most people would never have seen a fire demon, let alone had any idea how to defeat it."

Johanna spread her hands. "Then we hire magicians. Every ruler does it. I don't understand the problem. Anything has got to be better than sitting in this field. They act like they've got their feet stuck in tar. It's impossible to get them to do anything."

"They're not in a hurry to make decisions. They're comfortable—"

"They may be comfortable. They've got the best tents. They got first choice of the items the Baron lets us use. Many people aren't so lucky. Winter is coming." It had rained a lot recently, and the lower part of the field had become very muddy.

"I know, I know, child. You don't have to explain it to me."

Then why did he keep making excuses for these men?

Captain Arense and Joris DeCamp had come up behind them.

"I enjoyed that," the captain said, smiling at Johanna. He was a jovial fellow, with a huge beard, the typical ship's captain.

Joris chuckled. "Yeah, I don't think I've ever seen Ignatius Hemeldinck so restrained and angry at the same time. He's a piece of work, that one."

"Do not speak ill of other people," Shepherd Carolus said, coming up behind the Major and the Captain. "You never know when you need their help."

"Have a blessed day, Shepherd," Captain Arense said and gave an exaggerated bow.

"You jest, my friend."

Captain Arense clapped him on the shoulder. "Dirk, you are allowed to loosen up sometimes."

"I take my vocation seriously. Men who do not believe will watch like a cat and pounce when the opportunity arises. I'm the mouse. I try to stay out of their way. But like the mouse, I can go places where the cat can't come."

They all laughed.

Captain Arense said, "You, Dirk, look about as unlike a mouse as any person has ever looked."

"It is the metaphor that counts." He smiled and bowed. "But you have to excuse me, Your Majesty. I am expected to teach some children."

He continued along the riverbank and into the camp. Like a mouse. What a strange statement. She knew the nobles didn't particularly like the church, but was he suggesting there had been hostilities? She guessed that shouldn't surprise her, although making threats to a priest seemed tasteless to her, even a priest who was as apt to defend himself as the Shepherd Carolus.

Captain Arense said to Johanna, "We completely agree with you, by the way. We should make preparations to leave this field. I don't understand what is holding back the nobles, either. Maybe we'll find out, maybe we won't. I think you'd get quite a lot of support in the camp. Most people are sick of waiting for news that doesn't come. I'm rather sick of it myself. I'd rather be on the water. You should talk to my mistress about the use of the *Prosperity* for that reason."

That mistress was Julianna Nieland, Johanna's old rival, but the bite seemed to have gone off that rivalry, which had mostly concerned clothing and other trivial things. Like Johanna, Julianna had left her entire family behind in Saardam and hadn't heard a word from them since.

"I'll think about it," she said, still looking at Master Deim. His face didn't give away what he thought of such a plan.

"Would you know some adventurous young men who would like to go downriver to deliver a letter and check out what's going on in Saardam? We'll find a boat for them, and they can use two of our sea cows to come back upriver."

The animals in question grazed, as usual, in the shallows near the riverbank, where occasional bubbles rose to the surface. Sea cows seemed to like work.

"I think you'd find plenty of young men who would do that. Most youngsters are sick of being idle in this camp."

"Find names and recommend two to me."

The captain bowed. "It will be a pleasure, Your Majesty."

The men continued into the camp and Johanna walked with Roald and Master Deim up the gangplank of the *Lady Sara*. Two men stood on either side and they greeted the group with polite nods. They were supposedly royal guards, right now lacking a uniform. Johan Delacoeur had instated them *Because the royal family always has guards*, he'd said, and that was true, but suddenly Johanna wondered about these men and their motives.

They were ex-soldiers who Johan Delacoeur trusted and had served under him. But what if Johan Delacoeur's motives for posting the guards were not entirely honest? They might be employed to spy on the king as much as to protect him.

She hadn't thought to question it until now. Roald was the king and kings had guards, simple as that. Most of the men in the camp had little to do anyway, so guarding the king seemed a good thing to do. But Johan Delacoeur wasn't a friend, really, and he and his cronies had not been strong supporters of the royal family for quite a while.

Johanna, Roald and Master Deim stopped walking on the deck.

The day was brooding, and fat thunderclouds already gathered on the horizon. Pearls of sweat beaded on Master Deim's upper lip and forehead.

"It's very hot," he said, wiping his forehead. "There's a thunderstorm coming."

They watched the darkening sky in silence for a while. Even the birds seemed to be affected by the oppressing weather. One came strutting along the riverbank with its beak open.

"Look, a heron," Roald said. "You know they catch fish and frogs by spearing them with their beaks? The heron is from the sea-bird family, but do you know how far away from the sea we are? Isn't that strange?"

"Yes, very strange," Johanna said. They'd even seen seagulls the other day.

He went on to talk about other birds he saw. Larks, fluttering high in the sky, a pair of coots on the water, swallows skimming the surface so closely that occasionally their wings brushed the water, swifts in the sky, flying so high that you could hear their screeches only when you were very quiet.

Wouldn't it be amazing to be so lost in knowledge of birds and nature that you didn't see the terrible things that happened in life? Johanna met Master Deim's eyes.

"I'm so glad that you are here," she said. "You're a voice of reason, someone I know I can trust."

He sighed. "Not a word from your father or anyone else. I'm beginning to doubt the veracity of the claims in that letter. If the citizens of Saardam were well, certainly someone would have sent a letter, or someone else would have made the same journey up the river as we have, even if only to look for us."

Johanna had wondered the same thing. "Maybe they didn't come up the river far enough." Or maybe they, having seen the destruction of Aroden, had concluded that the whole world was dead. "The letter didn't actually say in so many words that the people were safe. It just said most of the citizens 'have been spared,' but it didn't say anything about their condition."

"It didn't. It's also strange how it mentioned business interests but not people. As if there was some sort of pre-arranged deal between Alexandre and the Baron about the spoils."

Johanna laughed in a hollow way. "And then he found that the King's coffers were empty, having spent all his money on the church."

"A nasty surprise, I'm sure. I wonder how much the Baron endorses this 'friend' Alexandre."

"I think Alexandre only calls the Baron a friend because he wants to be the Baron's friend. It seems to me that if he were really the Baron's friend, the Baron would have thrown the letter into the fire, and not given it to us even months after it was sent."

"True." Master Deim gave her a thoughtful look.

Something he hadn't considered, perhaps? "I'd really like to know what's going on in Saardam. I'm going to write that letter. I want to have it ready when Captain Arense finds some boys to go to Saardam."

He nodded and they stared over the churning water for a while.

Roald announced that he saw some ducks. He walked back down the gangplank past the impassive guards and kneeled, peering into the reeds. A young boy came to him, and Roald pointed. The boy kicked off his shoes and went into the water.

"The kids like him a lot," Master Deim said.

"Yes. They're not full of judgement, like adults." And Roald seemed to have remained stuck in that phase where boys find information interesting and want to learn about the world.

"True."

"Are you going to be at next week's meeting? I want to find volunteers to travel down the river to report on what's happening in Saardam."

"Just be careful. Don't anger the nobles. I haven't heard them say so, but they might well be disappointed that you survived. If that is so, I dare say they will try to get rid of you as soon as they can."

"They can't. I'm legally married to Roald."

"Yes, child, but I doubt they recognise the validity of the marriage. They may be patient for now, but that might change if you don't produce an heir soon."

CHAPTER 3

THAT DISTURBED Johanna more than anything, and as she watched Master Deim walk down the gangplank and wave to the guards with his usual jovial manner, a chill came over her. Because every night except those where she bled, she had slept with Roald and she had noticed no changes in her body. Her last bleeding was three weeks ago and it had disappointed her.

How long did it normally take for a woman to become with child?

She thought she had heard rumours that it had happened to some girls after being with a man just once.

Maybe she and Roald were doing something wrong.

A couple of young children were running between the tents, to a mother who had called them for the midday meal. All those people obviously knew how to do it right.

Was there anyone she could ask?

In Saardam, young women would ask Helena about being with men, about what to do the first time, about their husband's expectations, about how to tell when you were with child before you started swelling. But Helena, of course, had not been considered worthy to be taken on Captain Arense's ship.

That thought brought a pang of pain.

What would have become of Helena? Did sailors still come to Saardam and did they still have the money to pay to spend the night with her? Did young women still come to her with questions?

Johanna looked over the camp. The Captain was a supporter of the royal family and friendly to her, but he had taken far more men than women. The women who had made it onto the ships were mostly nobles. Johanna certainly wasn't going to ask them for advice—they'd be horrified to be asked about these things.

Roald's interest in books had provided him with access to the fabled library of the monastery of the Jeromist Order in town. Men with a love of books often formed bonds. He had a penchant for books of human anatomy, and in one of those she had spotted a drawing of a couple engaging in the reproductive act. The woman lay on her back and the man on top. That was how Roald had wanted it originally, but she found it uncomfortable. Maybe it was wrong for her to sit on top of him, because the seed came out as soon as she got up.

Maybe next time when she came to the library she should find some books on what she was doing wrong, or about magic or herb lore that she could use.

The stems threshed in the reeds and a boy yelled, "I got it! I got it!"

Two people waded through the reed bed back to the riverbank. First the boy, jumping up and down. Then Roald, carrying something in cupped hands. He climbed up the bank and walked past the guard up the gangplank. The man broke his normally impassive expression to frown at the thing in Roald's hands with a *good-heavens-what-now* look.

"For you," Roald said, slightly puffed.

In his hands he held a tiny fluffy brown and yellow duckling. It peeped.

In the water below, the mother duck quacked.

Roald couldn't have looked any less like a king had he tried. His pants were wet and muddy up to the knees and there was a green smudge on his cheek.

Johanna laughed. "I think it belongs with its mother."

Just then, that mother duck flew up onto the deck and walked, flat-footed in Roald's direction. She quacked and shook her tail. The duckling peeped.

"Put it down," Johanna said.

Roald bent. The duckling jumped out of his hands before he had lowered them onto the deck and scampered to its mother. The mother duck then flew back down into the water to the rest of her brood, and the little one jumped all the way from the edge, landing sideways with its little feet flailing, but bobbing back onto the surface.

Roald laughed.

Johanna went up to the cabin where she found Nellie in the galley and Loesie busy sewing while seated on a roll of rope in the shade of the cabin, with the summer breeze coming in through the open door.

Since Nellie had made this cabin hers, she had put up lace-edged curtains—from the underwear that they had taken from the burnt-out farm along the Saar River—and crocheted a bed spread from coarse wool which she had bought at the local markets.

Loesie was squinting at her work, and the tip of her tongue poked out between her lips in concentration.

Johanna laughed. "I didn't know you could sew, Loesie."

"I can't. She's teaching me," Loesie said. "I was bored. I can make apple baskets, but there's not many apple baskets to be made."

"And? Are you turning into a seamstress?" Johanna eyed

Loesie's work, by far less neat than Nellie's, which lay on the bed.

"Nah, not a chance. Give me some cows to milk any day."

"Are you ready for the midday meal, mistress?" Nellie asked from the galley.

"I think so. Bring it quickly before Roald runs off to catch some other animal."

"Yes, sure. I'll do it now."

Johanna sat on the hold cover, turning her face into the humid breeze. The sun had vanished behind the fuzzy edges of the top of the thundercloud that was coming closer at alarming speed. Squalls of wind tore at her clothes and already thunder growled in the distance.

Roald's catches had been an endless source of amusement. Over the past week, he'd brought a small rabbit, little fish in a jar and a tiny mouse. She didn't mind those so much, but drew the line at the frog he'd caught. She did *not* like frogs. They were green and wet and cold and—eeeeew.

He'd held up the frog enclosed in both his hands, with its head poking out, and told her all about its life cycle and about the different kinds of frogs. He had put it on the desk so that he could draw it—he was quite decent at drawing. Unfortunately, the frog had other ideas, so he'd spent the next hour chasing it around the hold.

Whatever you wanted to call Roald, he wasn't an idiot. He remembered things he read in books. He understood them, as long as those things were facts, as long as people left him alone with his books.

It was only now that she began to understand how stressful it must have been for him to speak to the highly critical nobles of Saardam at the ball and dance with strange girls who expected some kind of Prince Charming. He'd made inappropriate comments not because he was lewd, but because he was scared and didn't understand what people expected of him.

Nellie was just coming out of the galley with a tray when the first clap of thunder hit. She flinched and ducked, but managed to hang onto the tray.

"It's getting close, mistress."

They quickly made their way down the stairs, where Roald gave Johanna an alarmed look.

"Thunder," he said, his eyes wide. "The little duckies will be all right, won't they?"

"They'll be fine. They'll shelter in the reeds."

"But they'll get wet if it rains."

"They're ducks. They're used to getting wet."

Nellie put the tray down on the tiny table at the bottom of the stairs and left again, shutting the cover behind her.

"Dinner," Johanna said. She set the plates on either side of the table and uncovered the tray. Legs of rabbit, applesauce and carrots. The food smelled heavenly. How did Nellie manage to get all these things?

One of the things that worried her was that Roald tended to forget to eat if no one paid him any attention. He got distracted and somehow just didn't feel hungry. But he loved Nellie's applesauce, so she gave him a big dollop of that, some carrots and a good chunk of rabbit meat. For a while they sat eating happily.

The hold that had carried many a load of grain down the river and spices upriver was long and narrow. They had made a small sitting room near the stairs that had replaced the ladder. It held a carpet, a small table, two mismatched chairs and a tiny desk where Roald sat reading whenever he wasn't roaming the riverbanks. A fat book lay open there.

"What were you reading?"

"I'm reading a very interesting book about the night sky and the phenomena in the heavens. The writer says that there are other worlds like the Earth and that they all go around the Sun."

"Rinius."

He gave her a sharp look. "Yes. You know him?"

"No, but Father brought me a copy of that book." It was in her room, likely burned in the fire. The thought of her comfortable room and house constricted her chest. What would have happened to Father or Koby or Master Willems?

"It's very interesting. I like this book a lot. He says that the Moon is a world like ours and that people live there."

She laughed, remembering that last chapter of the book with its strange speculations. "Maybe, but I doubt we'd ever see them, if the Moon is really as far away as Rinius says it is."

"How far is that?" He turned around and reached for the book. He opened it at a page with diagrams. Johanna had studied them, but had to admit that she found Rinius' calculations hard going.

"Here it says." He pointed at the page and moved his finger down as he read. "It says that it is four hundred and twenty-eight times the length of the Saar River. That is a long way indeed."

"You couldn't travel that far."

His face went thoughtful. "You would have to get free from the Earth."

"What do you mean?"

"The Earth and the Moon are both worlds floating in the air. To get to the Moon, you have to free yourself from the Earth and cross the air."

"You mean fly? That's impossible."

"A bird could do it."

"People don't fly," Johanna said, uneasily. "Isn't there this story of a father and son who both strapped on wings, but the son flew too close to the sun so the wax that held the wings together melted and he fell down and died?"

"That's a myth. People can't fly when they strap on wings. They're too heavy. Birds have hollow bones and they're light."

"Then people can't fly."

"They could use a machine."

A what? Where did he get these ideas?

"The eastern traders have machines." He went on an extended explanation about these machines, which, apparently, ran on wood and steam and could make carts move by themselves, and could do things like saw wood and grind grain if there was no wind for windmills.

"But there is always wind."

"In Saardam there is, but not in the eastern forests."

Guess he had a point there. "Roald, listen. We have to be careful. Don't ever let Shepherd Carolus or the nobles hear you say things like this."

He gave her a blank look.

"Rinius' book is considered heresy by many in Saardam." Especially the Church. She also wasn't sure about the Belaman Church's position on the subject of Rinius. A large part of his book argued that the beliefs and gods were a figment of human imagination. Why a book like that would be owned by a monastery was beyond her.

"But what he says is true."

"True or not, nobody can prove it."

"Yes, we can go to the Moon and measure how far it is."

Sure. We can do that tomorrow. "Just be careful with the things Rinius says." Johanna sighed. "Your father was very close to the church. I'm not sure what went on just before the ball and just before you came back, but he didn't get on well with the nobles and they were very angry with him."

"Oh." Another blank look.

"Did he tell you anything about it?"

"Father said that if I became king, all the men were mine."

He really didn't understand. Where did that leave her? Alone and isolated. Without too many friends in this camp, or outside it.

In a way she was glad that the Baron had been conspicuous by his absence. She wasn't keen to speak to him and she could still hear the last words Sylvan had said to her about Kylian: *he's a necromancer*. Of course no one in the camp had mentioned anything about it, nor, fortunately, had she seen Kylian.

She hadn't been able to do anything about contacting the Magician's Guild, as Sylvan had suggested. Whenever she had been in town, she had looked for the guild, but Florisheim was a warren of narrow streets and slate-roofed houses that all looked the same. Somehow, she had expected the Magician's Guild to be easy to find, because this whole area was rife with magic, right?

Rife with magic, it certainly was. Often, a breeze would waft past that made her skin prick, despite her inability to see things in the wind. Often, too, she would see misty shapes lurk in the reed beds, only to vanish again when she looked closely. They were ghosts and other beings, and they were watching, ready to pounce.

She and Loesie were the only Saarlanders in the camp with as much as a shred of magic. If magic pounced, there would be no warning.

CHAPTER 4

B Y THE TIME Roald and Johanna finished their meal and Johanna went up to the deck, the sun had well and truly disappeared behind thick clouds. The sky towards the west had darkened to the colour of ash, leaden, almost dark blue. Gusts of wind whipped at Johanna's hair. Nellie rushed across the hold covers behind the cabin, where she pulled flapping sheets and shirts off the washing line before they blew into the water.

"It's sure going to rain, mistress." Her cheeks were red with the effort.

Nellie had to give up wearing a bonnet when her only one became too torn and dirty during their foray with the bandits and now wore her flaxen hair in a bun.

"I look like a peasant girl," she had complained.

That might be true, but a very healthy and good-looking peasant girl. Her skin was much better than Johanna's, her shape was better, and living on the ship had brought out a no-nonsense streak in her which Johanna liked. Through the terrible events that they'd experienced, Nellie had been unquestionably loyal. Nellie deserved to be married.

Loesie now also came out and helped Nellie. A squall of wind almost blew a sheet out of Nellie's hand. Both women scrambled to hold onto it, and then laughed.

At times like this, Loesie looked almost normal albeit still a bit dark for a Saarlander. Her skin bronzed a lot more, too. She had never regained her peasant's accent after the demon had been driven from her.

Loesie and Nellie now got along quite well, and Johanna wasn't sure what to make of that. The Loesie she knew from the markets in Saardam wasn't such an open, laughing creature. She was mysterious, she would deliberately frighten little boys, and sometimes bigger ones, who came to beg or tease her. She would pretend to curse young men making lewd comments to her. All of that was gone. Did people's characters change after they had been possessed by a demon?

A couple of fat drops started to fall, and Nellie and Loesie rushed back into the cabin. Nellie shouted to Johanna, "Better stay dry, mistress!"

While the first rain hit the covers, Johanna descended the narrow and steep steps into the hold, where Roald had settled in his usual chair with a book. He'd sit there all day if she let him.

She came up behind him and put her hand across the page.

He protested. "Hey! I was reading that."

"Roald, I need you to do something for me. It's a secret."

He turned around and his frank eyes met hers. "Oooh, I love secrets."

"Put on your peasants' shirt and trousers. We're going out." She cringed. His pants were still wet from this morning's escapade into the reeds. She hoped he wouldn't catch anything.

"But it's raining," he said.

"That's good. People will be inside." Although the rain

was really pelting down on the hold covers now. A clap of thunder made the ground shake.

Roald gasped and then he said, "It's all right. I'm only scared of thunder at night. We will stay away from trees. You know that if lightning hits a tree, you can die from the presence of the fire demon that comes down with the lightning?"

Just then a lightning bolt hit somewhere close, followed by a sudden clap of thunder.

Thanks, Roald, that's really helpful information right now.

In the semidarkness of the hold, Johanna searched for her peasant dress. Nellie had washed it since coming here, but every time she put it on she thought of the burned-out farm where they had found these clothes, and their bed sheets, and other things. It still felt like stealing, even though the blackened bodies of the woman and baby in the burned-out kitchen were unlikely to ever need these things again. She thought of the thriving vegetable garden outside, the poor cows bursting with milk, the ruined mill. And she thought about the ruins of Aroden castle and the nearby town, where people had run along the riverbank with the *Lady Sara* begging for help. How were those people coping now?

She pulled on the drab dress and then helped Roald get dressed in his decidedly damp trousers and, not much later, they climbed up the narrow staircase out of the hold. A good amount of rain came in when Johanna slid the cover aside. The drops were large and stung with cold.

There was another crack of lightning followed by rumbling thunder.

Roald gasped.

"It's only thunder," Johanna said, trying to cover her own unease.

"Yes. I'm not scared of thunder." But his eyes were wide. "It can't hurt you. Except when you're under a tree."

"Aren't we lucky that there are no trees between here and

the boat shed?" Nowhere to shelter either, and the rain was coming down in sheets. She could barely see the other side of the river.

"Is that where we're going? The boat shed? You know that there is a swallow's nest right up the top against the far wall?"

Johanna shut the cover and they ran across the deck to the gangplank. As quickly as she could, she let herself slide to the jetty and helped Roald.

A few more distant cracks and rumbles shook the ground. Johanna held her breath with each one. It was easy to pretend that you weren't scared of thunder when you were not in the middle of a storm, and this one was really getting very close.

Those sullen guards by the sides of the gangplank both stood hidden deep within the hoods of their army-issue cloaks.

"Are you going out in this weather?" one asked.

"No need to come. Roald is going to show me some frogs."

She hoped that excuse would work, although they would remember that fuss over the escaped frog, and know that she did not like frogs.

The men nodded.

They were sure to report to Johan Delacoeur that "the king and his consort" had gone out in the pouring rain for "catching frogs". That was not to be helped.

Johanna and Roald slipped and slid over the path along the riverbank. A squall of wind blew the rain in their faces.

A nearby thunderclap cracked through the sky and shook the ground. Roald yelped and dropped to his knees, holding his arms over his head.

"Are you all right?" Johanna pulled him up, feeling the tenseness in his muscles.

"Maybe we should go back. The thunder can harm you, right?"

"It's exciting, an adventure," Johanna shouted over the noise of the pelting rain. They were both soaked all over. Cold rivulets of water were running down Johanna's back.

The boat shed along the river was a dark shape against the grey sky. It was hard to see where they were going with water running in her eyes. The sudden snap of cold air made mist rise from the water. Was it her imagination or was there a peculiar smell to the air? Her imagination certainly didn't play tricks with her as far as the swirling shapes in the mist were concerned. The ghosts watched, and waited.

Inside the shed, it was almost too dark to see, but at least it was dry. The wooden table and benches where the nobles would sit for their meeting stood forlorn in the middle of the compacted earthen floor. The rain made such a racket on the roof that it would be impossible to hear if anyone came. Better be quick.

Johanna walked along the walls, looking up at the ceiling beams. "Here it is. Lift me up."

Roald lifted her by her waist, but she still couldn't reach the timber, only the rough clay of the walls.

"Not high enough. Can I stand on your shoulders? Wait."

She took off her shoes and then her overdress. Even the fabric of her underdress was so wet that it stuck.

Roald giggled and put his hands on her sides. She could feel the warmth through the soaked fabric. "It's a pity I can't look at you here."

"Not now. We have to do something first. I have to reach the ceiling." She tried to climb on him by pushing herself up on his shoulders. He held his hands together so she could put her foot in them to boost herself up, but she almost fell.

She let herself down. "It's too wobbly. Wait. I'll stand with my legs apart on the bench. Then you put your head in between and I'll sit on your shoulders. Then you stand up and I'll use the wall to climb up."

So it was done, and finally she stood on Roald's shoulders and she could reach the wooden beams in the ceiling. As soon as she touched the wood, the images rushed to her.

She heard a familiar voice, that of Ignatius Hemeldinck.

"I'll go and see him." He sat at the table in the shed with the two other nobles from the council. They were wearing the same clothes as in the meeting this morning and this discussion had probably taken place after Johanna, Master Deim, Captain Arense, Joris DeCamp and Shepherd Carolus had left the shed.

"Let me come with you," said Johan Delacoeur.

Ignatius snorted. "What? Don't trust me?"

"Well," Johan said, "You don't seem yourself lately. I've not known you to give in to a woman."

Ignatius' face twitched. "It just seemed best not to escalate it further."

"Since when have you ever said that? What is wrong with you, man?"

Ignatius glared across the table.

"I think we should all go." Fleuris LaFontaine said. "Remind him of the promises he made us."

"Just the three of us, right?" Ignatius said.

"Yes, that goes without saying. I don't trust the captain or the mayor. That merchant, too, is much too friendly to her. I was waiting for him to reveal all we've been talking about."

"Rest assured, the only reason he didn't do that in the meeting is that he has already told her everything."

"He knows nothing." This was Ignatius again. Then he snorted. "I have to admit that we don't know much more either. It's like that meeting with the Red Baron at the castle never happened. 'We'll keep you informed,' he said. I'm tired of waiting."

"I agree I'm sick of it. And now we have this woman who is far too probing, but she's right about this. I've been unhappy that the Baron seems to have forgotten about us. It's all very fine for us to make excuses, like 'He's too busy,' but they're excuses, nothing more. We don't even know if he really is too busy, because we haven't seen him. And I don't like this business any more than she does."

There were headshakes around the table.

Ignatius pushed himself up from the table. "No need to panic. Let's just say that it's time to go into town and employ my contacts."

"And what are you going to do? Magically make the Baron appear and parade him through the camp?"

Ignatius smirked.

"You're kidding, right?" Johan said.

"Nope. I think the time is right."

"You're crazy."

"Don't let anyone see you, especially the captain or that priest. Those two are everywhere," Fleuris said. "If she finds out, you'll never hear the end of it. She'll think she has made us nervous."

Johan said, "She already has. She's a lot smarter than most women."

Ignatius snorted. "Bah, a woman. Nattering, gossiping, seductive creature."

"Don't underestimate her."

"No woman can match me. No woman will rule me."

They rose from the table and left. Johanna slowly withdrew her hand from the ceiling beam. The vision faded for the semi-darkness of the shed.

Well, that was certainly interesting. Master Deim had been right. They had made secret arrangements with the Baron. Maybe she should try the other beam to see what it had to tell her. She reached out—

A huge thunderclap shook the ground and made the walls of the shed rattle. Roald squealed and ducked. Standing with her hand outstretched, Johanna lost her balance. Her foot slipped off Roald's shoulder. She tried to steady herself against the wall, but Roald stood too far away from it and she hadn't the strength to keep herself up. She fell. Roald toppled over under her weight and they ended up in a tangle of limbs on the dusty floor.

Oof.

She had landed with her head on Roald's chest. "Are you all right?"

"We fell." Roald started laughing. "We fell."

Johanna scrambled up, brushing dust from her under-dress, but as wet as it was, she ended up smearing dirt across it.

She started laughing as well. They were both so wet and dirty and looked so much like a couple of children who had been playing in the mud. And it was raining so hard outside that getting back to the ship involved yet another dunking.

"I haven't told you that I love you yet today," Roald said. He put his hands on her shoulders and met her eyes. His beard had been trimmed that morning. It seemed to have grown fuller recently, and despite his condition and the childish innocence of his mind, he looked not unattractive. "I love you."

He slid his hands up over her shoulders until he cradled her head in both hands. Johanna stroked his hair and the sides of his face. His beard scratched her palms. She pulled him closer until she could kiss his lips. He remained unre-sponsive, but when she pulled back, the expression in his eyes showed his interest.

"Maybe I could look at you now?"

"What? Here?" She eyed the shed's empty interior, the table and benches, the bare ground with gouges from where people had dragged boats that would now be on the water.

And would probably be filling up with water from the rain outside.

He pulled at her underdress and peeped inside through the gap between her neckline and her chest. "Ooh, I can see something."

Johanna laughed. Well, why not? People did sillier things than that. She slowly undid the buttons at the front. He tried to poke his hand in, but she slapped him away, teasing

As the thunder rolled over the banks of the Rede River, and the rain pelted on the roof of the shed—and found its way inside by the sound of the drip-drip-drip on the floor—they came together. Johanna clung onto Roald's sweaty body while the edge of the table bit into her backside. The thrum of the rain masked any noises, and she wasn't ashamed that there were some noises.

She wouldn't really be a queen in the eyes of those men unless she had a child.

When it was done, after Roald had done his *hunhh!* thing and they clung to each other breathing fast while letting the glow ebb, they got dressed and ran through the rain back to the *Lady Sara*. Nellie had started wondering where they were. She fussed over the wet clothes and having nowhere to dry them.

Johanna said, "That's why we wore the peasant clothes." She wondered if Nellie would recognise the smell of seed that had ended up all over the back of the underdress.

"Still, mistress Johanna, did you have to go out in this weather?"

Yes, she did have to go out, and the wood had told her useful things. The nobles were concerned about her influence. They had made some sort of deal with the Baron, and now the Baron was ignoring them. Why? Because the Baron had what he wanted and didn't need the nobles anymore? Worse: what was Ignatius Hemeldinck planning to do?

CHAPTER 5

WHEN CRACKS of daylight leaked between the hinges of the covers, Johanna could no longer stay in bed.

Roald was still asleep. He lay on his side, with his face to her, his eyes closed, little slivers of blond eyelashes. He was so peaceful that she didn't want to disturb him.

She got dressed as quietly as she could, took her basket with the leather cover and climbed up the creaky stairs. Roald groaned and turned over, but didn't wake up. A peek from underneath the heavy hold cover gave her a glimpse of wet boards and little circles where raindrops fell in a puddle.

Dang it. Still raining.

She crept down the creaky ladder again to get her woollen cloak.

Out on the deck of the *Lady Sara*, it was still very quiet. Not even Nellie and Loesie appeared to have risen. In the camp on the river bank, a few trails of smoke rose from people cooking breakfast, but not even the boys were out to play yet.

It must have rained a lot in the foothills of the mountains

because the river was high with muddy churning water. Sticks and bits of grass drifted downstream at a good pace. The drop from the deck to the jetty had increased quite a bit and the *Lady Sara*'s gangplank had become quite steep. She had to shuffle down carefully, holding the rope to make sure that she didn't slip.

At the riverbank, the guards stood hidden in the depth of their woollen cloaks, their hands in their pockets.

"What a miserable day," she said.

One of the men turned around sharply, as if she had startled him. "Good morning, mistress. It's a lousy day to be out."

"I have a need to visit the library to get some new books for Roald." She patted her basket, looking as innocent as she could. "He's getting bored."

She wasn't sure how convincing the excuse was on a rainy day like this; after all, the precious books might get wet. But on rainy days there was lots of time to read, as well, and he made no protest.

"Do you want someone to accompany you?"

"Thank you, but I'm fine with going alone. I know where the library is. And it would be a very boring place for you, I'd wager." Why were they asking this all of a sudden? They had never shown any concern for *her* safety. In fact, they'd mostly ignored her. Was it because of things she had said yesterday?

The man nodded. "As you wish, mistress."

Johanna drew the hood of the cloak over her head, debating if she should tell them to address her as *Your Majesty,* as was appropriate. But she didn't like this renewed attention from the men at all, and would do best not to push them.

She walked quickly over the path between the tents, looking down so she didn't step in the puddles. Some of them were very deep, and already parts of the field were becoming sodden with the high water in the river.

The field of the camp lay in an outer curve of the Rede

River. The path that led to the boat shed continued upstream through a swampy thicket with willow trees. Someone had put two rows on logs on the ground and filled up the space between them with sand to make a path, but today, even that was half-flooded, so Johanna had to walk past the back of the swamp, where the little path went up the levee where it joined the main road into town.

The town of Florisheim lay stretched out along the eastern bank of the Rede River, snug between the water and the forested hills. Those hills were too steep to build on, she'd been told, so the town took up only the somewhat less steep riverbanks and the lower part of the slopes.

Because of its strategic position along the river, Florisheim was foremost a fortress town, with thick city walls as the first line of defence. The quay, in the bend of the river, was a plain, barren place, with another forbidding wall at its back and a single gate that provided entrance to the city. There were also a couple of entrances at water level, closed off by heavy iron gates, now half covered in muddy, churning water.

Baron Uti's castle stood on the highest point within the walls, an ancient, menacing building, having thick walls with slits for the guards to shoot their arrows. If you came in from a certain angle, you could see the top of a catapult poking in between the parapets. The castle had one fat and stumpy tower on the corner overlooking the town. The main gate was in the western wall, next to the tower, and the castle was separated from the rest of the town by a drawbridge over a little creek that ran from the hills into the Rede River.

Johanna entered the town through western city gate, where a bored sentry looked miserable under his wet cloak.

The town's houses were mostly made of clay-daubed wood, painted white or red, while the wooden framework was painted black. The patchwork walls made neat patterns that, today, were darkened with rain that was again increasing. The streets were almost entirely a single, muddy puddle. Water dripped off the straw roofs. Smoke curled from chimneys and hung low over the town, spreading tendrils of fog and the scent of burnt wood and cooking. Most people stayed indoors by the fire and she met only a goose-herder boy driving a flock of ten or so birds, which waddled ahead of him, with their orange feet going splash, splash, splash in the puddles.

Johanna picked her way through the narrow and winding streets. Since arriving at the camp, she had come into town a number of times, usually to visit the markets or the bakery, but occasionally the barber or tailor, and she knew the way. Today, it was so early that a lot of the shops hadn't opened, and the market vendors hadn't set up all their wares. In fact, it looked like many weren't going to be here today.

One side of the market square was dominated by an elaborate stone building with a belltower. It had pillars with carved gnomes and trolls and gargoyles on the corners. There were little winged devils and ugly faces. It was, of course, the main building of the Belaman Church, and she had walked past, gazing at the stained glass window many times, wondering what it would be like from the inside. People had told her about its splendour.

Today, the elaborate doors stood open and the sound of singing drifted to the street. A choir of young voices, singing in beautiful harmony. Johanna climbed the few steps to the porch and entered a dark foyer that gave access to the main church hall. A broad aisle with mosaic tiles went to the front, where there was a stone altar, also with elaborate carvings on the side that faced the many rows of pews. The Belaman Church did not depict their god. It believed that each person held the god in their hearts and pictures of a bearded man, like the one in the Church if the Triune, were unnecessary. The wall behind the altar held a huge mural of a hand that appeared out of the clouds, and this hand was the only part of the god that made it into paintings. It pointed an index finger at the sun, which cast brilliant rays of light in response. The sun and its rays were painted in gold and the sky in radiant blue. All along the edges of the mural, there were flowers and vines with fruit, and ears of grain heavy with seed.

Wow, she'd never seen a church this big, or this beautiful.

A bunch of choirboys stood on tiered stands and the choirmaster was talking to them, his voice echoing in the emptiness.

Immediately inside the hall stood tiered tables with hundreds of candles. Tall ones, stubby ones, white ones, carved ones and coloured ones, all of them with flickering, flapping, smoking flames. The faint scent of soot and wax laced the air.

High in the walls at both sides were windows of brightly coloured glass. One depicted a trio of men lifting their hands to a bright light in the sky. The colours were beautiful, bright and clean. Amazing reds, oranges, yellows and greens. The brightest of blues. Purple even. Didn't they make that dye from some sort of shell?

The church was so big that, besides the central aisle, there were two more aisles between the rows of pews and the outer walls. Johanna walked to the one on her right, past the many rows of candles, which flapped more vigorously in her wake.

Each candle came with a little sign made from parchment or cheaper paper. She bent over to read the curly script. Names, mostly. Of people who had passed away, she guessed. One card had flowers drawn on. Another a young woman's face. A lot of cards had been written in the same hand, probably written by a church attendant on behalf of mourners.

While she stood there, the choir started to sing again, and the voices of young boys filled that giant hall with a hymn in chilling harmony. Johanna's skin puckered into goose bumps.

She walked past huge paintings of giant men with wings, and statues on pedestals. At the base of some, people had put bunches of flowers. The Belaman Church might not depict their god, but they sure loved their many saints. Some statues were old and plain, others elaborately painted. But even the old ones—and one of the statues was very old and worn, as well as greasy from the touch of many hands—had elaborate pedestals and velvet-covered benches for worshipers to kneel and pray.

If King Nicholaos had spent a lot of money on the Church of the Triune, it was a mere drop compared to the flood of money this church must have at its disposal.

The final statue in the row was a white marble life-sized figure of a woman. She wore a long cloak, held her hand, palm up as if begging, and had her face turned to the sky. The hood of her cloak half-covered her hair. She looked quite young and was also visibly pregnant.

This statue was surrounded by a stepped pedestal, and every step was covered in flowers, little toys, some baby socks even. Each one told a little story of itself. Of lost children, of children hoped-for or mothers lost in childbirth. Johanna looked for, but didn't see, a sign with the saint's name.

She sat on one of the benches surrounding the shrine, jamming her hands between her knees.

The voices of the choir rose into a crescendo, a multitude of harmonies.

In her imagination, the marble woman saint looked at the sky and pleaded *please, grant me a child. Only one will do and I care not if it is a boy or a girl.*

In her imagination, she knelt on the steps and prayed.

Certainly, it was not proper to pray in a church that wasn't yours?

A male voice said, "I would not have expected to see you here, child."

Johanna gasped. She hadn't heard the brother come up from behind. He was very tall, with a short stubble of hair on his head.

Johanna rose. "I'm sorry. I didn't mean to trespass—"

"No one trespasses when they come into the house of the Lord. All are welcome." He spoke with faint eastern accent. "I'm Brother Velespius, and it honours me to have you as a guest in our church."

"But I'm not a member."

"I know who and what you are. All are welcome in the church, day or night. It's never too late to pray to the true God and convert."

"I think I already believe in the true God."

"Do you?" He fixed her with an intense look. His brown eyes held an intense expression that made her feel uneasy.

"I think we all believe in the same God, because we are all people of the same land. We all know what is good and what is bad."

"You have a very generous spirit."

The choir had stopped and the choirmaster was yelling something at the boys about going to the midday meal.

"They are very good," Johanna said.

"People come from far and wide to listen to the choir. It's an honour for those boys to be in it. The abbot travels the country to scout for good voices. I was a member of the choir myself, but that was many years ago."

"You've lived in the monastery ever since?"

"Yes. I was a teacher and scribe before becoming a librarian and running the printing press."

Johanna looked up at the marble face of the young saint. "Who is this woman?"

"She is the holy saint Magdalena, the mother of all mankind. Women come here to pray for a child, for an easy delivery or to pray for children they have lost. Am I guessing that this is the reason you have come here also?"

"Um . . ." How did he know this? "I came because I walked outside and I heard the singing. It was so beautiful that I had to come and listen."

"While you're here, do pray to Saint Magdalena. She is the saint of mothers and motherhood. I'm thinking you will be joining that group soon."

CHAPTER 6

JOHANNA ENDED UP making a short prayer to Saint Magdalena. The Brother seemed friendly and she couldn't see the harm, because they were all part of the same church, right? If Saint Magdalena was fair, she would look kindly upon every woman, not just those who lived in town.

She left the church again not much later, unsure what to think of it. The singing was beautiful, but while the display of wealth was very pretty, it seemed unfair to her, and she disliked the suggestion that she should convert. Why should these people care? It was all these same church.

The library belonged to the old monastery next to the castle, which had a water mill feeding off the same creek that ran underneath the castle's drawbridge. The monks made paper and operated a bookbindery on the ground floor. The back of the building held a huge collection of books, which she'd been told had belonged to a former abbot with a love of the written word who had bequeathed his collection to the order.

Johanna went in through the huge double doors with the

snake-headed door handles. In the foyer, the familiar old monk sat writing at a small table by the light of a flapping candle. A proper wax candle it was, too, one that would not produce as much greasy soot as the tallow candles. He wrote on a large sheet of thick parchment, beautiful letters in intricate strokes. Right now, he was colouring in the margins with lines of blue and red, a true work of beauty.

He nodded a greeting to Johanna without lifting his head from his work. The light from the candle reflected in the bald skin on top of his head.

He said, "He's in the paper press room."

The "he" would be Brother Reginald, the monk who looked after the library.

She went through the room to the left, where the rattling and clanking and creaking sounds of a working mill were loud. A couple of monks worked here, scooping ground-up cloth onto mesh sieves. The resulting layer of fluff in the bottom of the sieve would be press-dried into paper. It was noisy in the room with the constant rattle of the giant wheels and shaking of the sieves. It was stuffy in here, too, even though the door was open.

She continued through to the main room, where a couple more monks greeted her with nods. Both wore drab grey habits, tied at the waist by a simple rope. The older one was Brother Reginald.

"The day is blessed, lady," he said. Johanna had grown used to his thick accent and strange turns of phrase.

With the wrinkled skin that hung off his face and arms like an ill-fitting suit, Brother Reginald looked older than time itself. But his eyes were sharp, and the expression in them not nearly as old and tired as his body suggested.

Johanna laughed. "I've certainly seen more blessed days than this. The weather is awful. Does it often rain like this?"

"Not oft-times. The sun will come out again soon and you

will beg for the rain to come back." He placed his hands at the edge of the table and pushed himself up from his desk. "Has your husband finished his books again? He reads a lot, certainly."

"He does. He is a wise man." In case they thought Roald was stupid. "I will return the other books when it has stopped raining."

"There is no hurry. What would he like to read now?"

"Do you have any books on magic and herb lore?"

That earned her a wary look.

"He is interested in the plants and their properties." Last time she'd asked for books on the heavens so this was not too much of a stretch, she hoped. Roald *was* very interested in how nature worked.

"Herb lore, I can give you, although you had better ask the herb women in the markets. Magic is the domain of the Magician's Guild. We are a monastery." Brother Reginald's voice was prim.

"I was told that the Belaman Church allows magic. I'm sorry if I'm wrong. I don't know much about it. I'm after the magical properties of herbs."

"The church allows only certain magics, such as the magic of the holy spirit. That magic is considered sacred and the domain of men of the church. It is not the same as herb lore."

"Isn't herb lore magic?"

"No, not at all. Herb lore is the domain of herb women."

All these different definitions of magic were getting very confusing. "That means that you would have books on it?"

"We have some on herb lore."

"And magic?"

"Yes, we do have some of those, but we keep them locked away for the sake of safety of our citizens. Magic is a dark, evil subject, and people would do well not to meddle with it."

"I only wanted herb books for my husband."

He gave her a thoughtful look and stroked his beard. His eyes had an *I-don't-believe-you* look in them, but to her surprise, he nodded. "All right. Come with me."

He led her up a narrow winding staircase with uneven steps that came out in another large room filled with books. Between the two floors and the downstairs bookbindery, Johanna had never seen so many books in one place. At home, Father owned a few cabinets of books. That was considered a treasure. She hated to think how much all these books were worth. That abbot must have spent all his life collecting them.

Brother Reginald began pulling books off the shelves. He spread all of them out on a large table in the middle of the room. Johanna opened some of them and turned a few pages.

There were books about the different herbs and where they grew. There were books with intricate coloured-in drawings of plants. One book contained maps of places where these plants grew. Roald would love this.

She wondered where the magic books were hidden. She could see another winding staircase through a door across the room from where they'd entered.

A man's voice called downstairs.

Brother Reginald put another couple of books down. "If you will pardon me, I have to talk to a customer about his paper that we're making." He winked. "We wouldn't let the mayor wait, now, would we?"

He went back down the stairs and the sound of jovial voices drifted up.

How are you today?

Never better.

That sort of thing.

Johanna waited, leafing through the books on the table. Brother Reginald and his customer appeared to have moved into the papermaking room.

It was amazing how many books were here. The shelves covered every bit of wall in the room. Leather-bound books with gold-embossed titles; thinner volumes with paper covers; large, heavy books; small, fat books. Books in numbered series, books in languages she couldn't read and some in languages she didn't even recognise.

While she stood there, she noticed movement in the corner of her eye at the top of the staircase. Someone was coming up the stairs and she had been so absorbed in all these books that she hadn't even heard footsteps.

But the slender figure that came out of the stairwell wasn't Brother Reginald. It was a woman in a heavy cloak with the hood pulled over her hair, her face hidden within the shadow of the fabric.

Johanna was about to say something, but the words died on her tongue at sight of the woman's sickly pale hand. She had heard that there was a disease in this region that disfigured people's faces. Would this woman be suffering from it?

The woman didn't look up or seem to notice Johanna at all. She crossed the room, gliding around the table in the middle as if she barely touched the ground. Her footsteps made no sound even though the floor was made of wood. For a moment, Johanna thought she was a ghost, but she looked far too solid.

Yet the tingle of magic wafted in her wake.

The woman went to the entrance to the second staircase and disappeared up the steps and out of sight. A glow of light flickered into being on the floor above, casting a golden triangle of light on the wall in the staircase.

Were the magic books up there?

Brother Reginald was still talking to his customer. Their voices echoed from one of the rooms downstairs, mingled with the rattling and clanking of the mill wheels.

As silently as she could, Johanna crept up the stairs.

The light from the flapping candle flame cast long shadows over the wall. The stone was pitted and the wall was curved, so the shadows were rough and distorted, making it hard to see where the woman was and what she was doing up there.

Johanna crept up a step, and another one, until the room came into view. As she had expected, this was yet another room full of books, except this one was much messier than the one downstairs, with books stacked on top of each other and on the floor.

The woman stood looking at the shelves. She held both her hands on the back of a chair. The skin was very pale, but unaffected by disease. She looked quite young.

Johanna wasn't sure what to do. She could talk to the woman, but she might not understand her. If she was important, Brother Reginald would have introduced her. If she wanted to speak to Johanna, the woman would have introduced herself.

Maybe—and she felt cold—this woman was the abbot's personal plaything. That was an embarrassing thought, but something she'd sadly come across more times than she cared to remember. She never knew who she felt more sorry for: the poor girl or the man who couldn't get a girl in any way other than to "buy" a poor wrench and feed and clothe her in return for certain services.

Anyway, she'd better go down before the Brother came back.

But as Johanna retreated a step down the stairs, the woman turned around so that the light fell on the side of her face. The straw-blond curly hair that poked out from under the hood was familiar. The freckles were familiar, too, and so were the dark blue eyes.

It was Princess Celine.

Johanna had never forgotten Celine's face. There was a

painting in the church hall that was an exact likeness of the princess as she had been just before her death. This woman matched the likeness down to the little mole on her cheekbone, down to her pale yellow dress with the tiny buttons and the lace frills.

She raised her hand to her mouth to stifle a gasp. That was impossible. The princess had been dead for a number of years.

"Ah, little princess," the woman said in a voice that sounded like the rasping of millstones.

Johanna wanted to run, but she couldn't. She stood petrified on the stairs, and might even have fallen had there not been the wall at her back.

"You have a problem, right, little princess?" The apparition laughed, a breezy sound.

Johanna retreated. Whatever this *thing* was, princess Celine, it was not.

"Come on, answer me."

Ghosts never talked to anyone. Sometimes they imitated a voice, but they never recognised people, they just went about their ghostly business without regard for who watched them.

"Tell me, what is your problem? Why have you come to the library?"

An ice-cold draught made the candles flap. It was so dark up here that if the flame blew out, Johanna wouldn't be able to see her way back down.

The apparition laughed again. "I'm going to have so much fun with this. Go on, try to take all the herbs and other quackery. Raspberry leaves, stinging nettles. Make the tea and drink it every night. That's why you're here, right? To see what you are doing wrong? To see why the idiot prince cannot get you with child. Keep trying. Go and stand upside down after he has fucked you. It will not help, but it will be good to see your despair. The reason is: because you're cursed by the deepest, darkest magic there is. You can never take the place that is rightfully mine. They will never accept you as their queen, because I am the queen!" She laughed, a horrible rasping sound.

"Get away from me! You're not real," Johanna yelled.

"I'm not real? Do you want to feel the cold of my curse?" She floated towards the top of the stairs, threatening to come down into the stairwell.

Johanna did her best not to scream. She launched herself down the stairs as quickly as she could, but the steps were narrow and uneven. She tripped, fell against the curved wall and tumbled a fair way.

The apparition whooshed past her with a rush of freezing air, leaving the sound of evil laughter in its wake. Johanna sat with her arms covering her head until she was sure that it was gone.

Her heart thudded like crazy.

Ouch, her wrist.

When she stumbled back into the other room, Brother Reginald just came running to the top of the stairs and stood there panting. He was not young, and many of his age would have given up climbing stairs long ago.

"What was all that noise?" His gaze rested on Johanna's arm.

Johanna looked. She was bleeding.

Oh. "I . . . fell down the stairs." She glanced at the entrance to the stairwell, but there was no sign of the apparition.

"Not much point being curious, young lady." He panted for breath. "There is nothing up there but spiders."

"That's not true. I saw—"

"That's just Liesel. She is always harassing people. She is harmless."

"Liesel?"

"Liesel the house ghost comes out sometimes when she is curious. She was the daughter of the original owner of this house, who gave it to the Order. She threw herself out of the tower window because of a spurned love affair. Don't those women all go funny when they think a man loves them?" He chuckled.

"But this was not a ghost. She was touching the chair. She was talking to me. She was looking at the books."

"There are no books up there. No chair either. You must have taken a spell."

Johanna looked from his bony frame to the entrance to the stairwell. She had *not* imagined this.

"I see you have doubts. Go upstairs. You'll see."

Johanna did.

The stairs came out into a dusty attic where cobwebbed items of furniture stood spread out in a haphazard way. There were no shelves with books, no desk with a chair, no piles of books on the floor, no candle, no table and no young woman.

That was the strangest thing ever. The library room had felt real. It had smelled real.

When she came down, Brother Reginald was nodding at her shocked expression. "It is a strange thing, and if I'd known that she was in this part of the building, I wouldn't have left you alone. Ah, Liesel, why do you make our lives so difficult?"

"Does she ever speak to everyone?"

He shook his head. "She doesn't speak at all. Not that anyone has ever heard."

"But she spoke to me . . . I don't think I saw the same ghost."

He gave her a brief *dumb woman* look, and she decided to leave the subject. The back of her neck pricked as if the ghost were still hanging around in the shadows.

From the table, Johanna chose a few books with pictures and lots of diagrams. Roald spent a long time figuring out text, but he loved illustrations and he was very good at deciphering their meaning, too.

She thanked Brother Reginald and left the library again, without books on magic, and without any potions to solve her problem.

CHAPTER 7

EVEN WHEN SHE was in the street, Johanna felt the eyes of Celine's ghost on her. She heard that raspy voice *You will never take the place that is rightfully mine*, which chilled her to the core of her bones. Why had Brother Reginald thought this was the ghost of a common girl? That did not look like a common girl to her at all. Her hands were clean and unblemished and unscarred from manual work. Her clothes were rich, with little pearl shell buttons and embroidery that common people couldn't afford.

She didn't look like a ghost, she didn't behave like a ghost. Yet she was not Celine, but someone's magical minion.

Johanna clutched the basket and made her way down the streets.

She didn't dare go back to the camp. The camp was full of Saarlanders who were unused to open displays of magic.

Some of the rich and influential people were said to believe that Celine was still alive and had been hidden away from the people to keep her pure. Those people said that the grave was empty and that the king's grief was a farce.

She checked over her shoulders many times and saw nothing except the wet street. But the trouble with a ghost was that if you didn't see it, that didn't mean it wasn't there.

It would be watching her and following her wherever she went and whatever she did. Watching and waiting for revenge. The nobles might even blame Johanna for bringing magic back to the camp.

Master Deim's family's house was in one of the higher streets of the town, close enough to the castle for the walls to loom menacingly over the roof.

When Johanna knocked, an adolescent girl opened the door and said something that Johanna didn't understand.

"I'm here to see Hieronymus Deim," she said.

The girl frowned and then repeated Master Deim's first name with such a different pronunciation that Johanna would never have picked it up if she'd heard it in a conversation on the street. The girl beckoned for her to come inside. She preceded Johanna through the dark corridor and into a warm living room where a number of people sat by the fire: a grey-haired woman with embroidery work sitting next to an oil lamp, two young boys playing on the floor, a man in his middle age—Master Deim's cousin?—and a woman of the same age. His wife or Master Deim's wife?

The merchant's eyes widened when he saw Johanna.

"Look at you. What brings you here in weather like this?"

He rose and took Johanna's hands in his. His skin felt like it was on fire. She hadn't realised up until now just how cold she was.

"Child, you look like you've seen a ghost. What's wrong?"

"Master Deim, please, I need to talk to you." And she *had* seen a ghost.

On the wall above the fireplace hung a large painting of the harbour of Saardam. Johanna recognised the work of the artist Claudius Verbeeck, whose commissioned works graced the walls of the town hall in Saardam.

His portraits of important Saarlander men were stiff and their likeness dubious at best, but his landscapes were beautiful, done in tiny little brush strokes and displayed so much detail that she could see Father's office. Was one of the ships in the harbour the *Lady Sara* or *Lady Davida*?

Then a disturbing thought: how many of these old buildings had survived the fire? The palace loomed over the houses. That was definitely destroyed. Probably a lot of the very old houses, too.

The middle-aged woman saw Johanna looking at it. "We will rebuild it," she said in slightly stiff but perfect Saarlander dialect.

Johanna turned to her. "You're from Saardam?"

As Johanna met the woman's eyes, the woman dropped to her knees. "My name is Hilda. I came from Saardam when I was young and beautiful. My family is at your service, Your Majesty."

It was the first time that someone addressed her like this and it took Johanna by surprise. She wanted to tell the woman to get up and stop being silly, but knew it was absolutely the right thing for her to do. Roald needed support as a king, and that meant people should treat him as a king. She said, "Thank you. I will do what I can, too, but it may take a while so you may have to be patient."

"We can be very patient. Whatever it is we can do, let us know. I will send my sons to fight, if they're old enough."

The young boys looked up from their game, clearly well-versed in the language.

"Thank you."

It was a strange and emotional moment to have someone promising her the life of her sons. The idea of going back to Saardam to free the city with an army abhorred her, but it might be what needed to be done. Although how an army could defeat strong magic wasn't clear to her.

"Actually, you can do something for me right now. I need to visit a woman who is well-versed in herb lore."

"You must go and visit Magda. She is simply the best."

Master Deim said something to her in the local language, and she replied in a somewhat annoyed tone.

Master Deim snorted.

"My brother-in-law says that Magda is an old witch."

"I can tell her that myself, and she *is* an old witch. Hilda, I know you don't have a shred of magic in you, but that woman is not half as harmless as she looks."

"She is the best. If you need her, you will find her house on the other side of the markets. It's a grey house, a bit dirty-looking, and there are strange things on the windowsills, but don't let that, or the sight of her face, frighten you."

Master Deim still didn't look happy about it.

"But will she understand me?" Johanna asked. She wondered what could be wrong with Magda's face.

"She will, even though she will grump about it, and pretty much everything else, too. Always making out that whatever you've asked is a big deal. She's not an inviting person, but just ignore the complaining. She'd be complaining a lot more if no one came. She'll know who you are, too, but she'll be rude about it—"

Master Deim said, "Hilda . . ."

She glanced at him. "What? I'm just warning the queen."

"Thank you," Johanna said.

"It is a pleasure." The woman curtsied and that was even more embarrassing than being called Your Majesty.

Master Deim snorted and led Johanna into the corridor, where it was very dark and cold.

The floor was covered in worn tiles that seemed to have been untouched for the last hundred years.

"This is a very old house," he said. "This part of Florisheim goes back all the way to the time of the Belaman invasion. Florisheim stood strong against their armies."

The Belaman religion had been much more successful.

Master Deim led her to the end of the corridor, up a narrow staircase and through a small doorway. It came out into a large room with windows along the far side that looked out over the slate roofs of the town and, beyond that, the river. Drops of water ran over the outside of the glass panes. All the roofs were dark and glistening with rain. The river had broken its banks in the low-lying areas on the opposite side, which was in Burovia.

"Look at all that water," Johanna said.

"It rained a lot in the foothills yesterday. There will be more to come. Those Burovian farmers should get their animals to higher ground."

A couple of cows stood on a patch that had become an island. They all faced the same way, with their backsides into the wind.

"Isn't that the religious order's land?"

"Not that," he said. "They own everything you can see to the north of here, but not further upstream."

"Who lives there?"

"No one. It's wild land and forest as far as the eye can see."

Johanna stood so close to the window that her breath fogged on the glass.

Forest with magical creatures, good and bad. She had only seen small parts of the forest, even when riding through with the bandits; there were always lone farmhouses and tiny villages along the way. *Forest as far as the eye can see* was not something she could comprehend. She didn't like forests. After her trek to Duke Lothar's castle and his explanation about magic lines, she liked it even less.

Master Deim said, "There are mountains to the south of the forest and other strange lands on the other side of those mountains."

"Father often told me about the strange lands and people there." He had not travelled there himself, but those people travelled up the rivers to Lurezia and he did business with them there.

"Have a seat."

Johanna sat on one of the cloth-covered chairs. Along the walls stood many wooden shelves filled with books, big leather-bound volumes and cheaper board-covered texts.

"I didn't know you had this many books."

"Many of them came from my brother's collection. This is his house."

"I thought the man in the living room was your cousin. I didn't know you had a brother."

"He is my cousin. I had a brother. He used to run half of our business, but he went to a trip down south and never returned."

"What happened?"

"No one knows. We never heard from him again. For this trip, he had chosen not to travel on one of the company ships, because he intended to travel south of the rapids. He was not alone, but rode with our company accountant. Neither of them were ever seen again."

"That must be a terrible thing to have happen."

He nodded. "Hilda is devastated. I'm helping her out with the boys. I'll probably end up marrying her." Master Deim's wife, she remembered now, had died a few years ago from wasting sickness. He told her that she'd already been thin when they married. Not even the best medics had been able to stop it. They never had children.

That thought made Johanna shiver. Some women just

never had children. Maybe there was something wrong with her.

There was a knock on the door and the maid came in with a tray with tea. Johanna and Master Deim were silent while she set out the cups and plates. Master Deim only spoke when the maid left.

"So what happened this morning that has you so out of sorts?" he asked while sitting down.

"It's a bit of a story. I went to the library to get new books for Roald to read."

"It's an odd time to go to the library."

"I know, but he ran out of books, and it's raining so he's driving me crazy doing nothing and fidgeting. Brother Reginald took me up to the library room. He was called away and while I was waiting for him to come back, and leafing through the books that he was going to give me, a ghost came up the stairs."

"Oh, that's Liesel. Everyone knows her."

"It was not Liesel. It was Celine."

He frowned at her. "Are you sure of that?"

"I know what Celine's face looks like. It was Celine. She was wearing that pale yellow dress with the tiny buttons that she wears in the painting of her that hangs in the church." She had to check herself. By all accounts, the Church of the Triune in Saardam had burnt to the ground. "Celine went up into another tower room that was also full of old books. She spoke to me. Her voice was like rasping millstones, not human at all. She said that I was a usurper and that only she could be queen."

His frown deepened. "Ghosts don't normally speak."

"No, they don't. They don't look solid either."

"Are you sure it was a ghost?"

"No, but it was some sort of magical apparition. After she'd made her threats to me, I ran down the stairs and fell.

Then Brother Reginald came back up from talking to his customer. I told him what I'd seen and he said there was no library room up there. I went back upstairs again and it was just an attic with lots of dust and spider webs. The ghost or apparition created an illusion around itself that was strong enough for me not to notice that it wasn't real."

He shook his head, the expression on his face worried. "I have never heard of anything like that."

"No, I haven't either. That's why I need to see a magician. Do you know that there are rumours that there is a necromancer in town?"

For a moment, an uneasy expression hovered in his eyes. He didn't deny the question. He didn't confirm it either.

"Hmm." He rubbed his chin and then repeated, "Hmm. Let me make some inquiries for you. But please don't go and see that woman Magda. She's harmless to people like my sister-in-law who just come to buy herbs, but her knowledge goes much deeper than that. She's rumoured to have been an accomplice for Duke Lothar's attempted poisoning of his half-brother. I presume you know about that."

She nodded. "Roald knows all these things. He's like a walking compendium of royalty."

Master Deim raised his eyebrows. "Is he, now?"

"Like you told me to do with Magda, you shouldn't underestimate him. He sits and reads all day, and he remembers all of it. He's just really awkward with people. He doesn't like meetings and doesn't like to be in the spotlight."

"Hmm." He let a small silence lapse. "All right, I guess I shall keep that in mind then. But I repeat: don't see Magda. She is not just a herb woman."

"What if the reason I wanted to see her is just for herbs?"

He seemed taken aback by that statement. "Oh. Sorry. Just for herbs, then, but I would prefer if you bought them from any other herb seller at the markets, if you can."

"I will try." But Johanna was curious about this Magda now. If she was a friend of Duke Lothar's then she might have useful information. No matter what people said about the duke, he was the only one to have given her serious information about magic and the only one to have helped her with the matter. She didn't want to take sides between the Duke and his half-brother Baron Uti, but the Duke at least had taken her seriously, even if she was only a woman, while the Baron had so far done his best to ignore her.

Master Deim repeated his promise that he would talk to someone about the apparition of Celine, and repeated his warning against Magda a third time.

Then she asked him the question that she had never dared ask when they both still lived in Saardam. "Do you have some magic?"

He hesitated only a moment. "I do. I have very limited water magic. The water in the tea tells me that the young maid who opened the door for you has been kissing the neighbour's coachman in our kitchen again. I'll have to talk to her about that. He's from a family that's no good, and if she keeps going like this, she'll end up in trouble and then she'll have to marry him."

Johanna wondered why so many young women got *in trouble* while she could not end up *in trouble* no matter how often she and Roald shared the bed.

"The water in the river tells me how much it has rained upstream."

"Do raindrops tell you what it's like to fly?"

He frowned at her like he'd never considered that angle. "I guess they could. How did you come up with that thought?"

"Roald. He says a bird could fly to the Moon by crossing the air."

"He's been reading Rinius." It was not a question.

"Yes. He's fascinated by all those things."

"You are aware that most churches consider Rinius heresy? The Church of the Triune is one of those churches. Your father often lamented that you went to it."

"There are more reasons than one to attend a church. I liked how the church teaches that people are equal regardless of their wealth. I like how they help poor and unfortunate people. I don't like their position on magic. I'd like Saardam to be a place of free thought and inquisitive minds."

The more she thought about it, the more convinced she became of this. The crime was not that Rinius had some strange ideas. It was that he had been hanged for voicing them.

CHAPTER 8

B Y THE TIME Johanna left Master Deim's house, the rain had intensified and didn't look like letting up any time soon. The sky was leaden grey and wind lashed at trees.

She ran through the narrow streets, empty except for puddles, through the gate, where the bored sentry still sat being miserable in his little hut, and along the by now very muddy path to the camp. The books made her basket heavy. The wind kept pulling at the leather covering. She must have eaten something bad because her stomach cramped.

At the camp, some people were still attempting to cook dinner, but even the wood that had been stored under shelter was wet, and most refugees hid inside their tents.

The gangplank of the *Lady Sara* had become even steeper and slipperier than when she left.

When she opened the hold cover that provided access to the stairs, a good amount of rain came in. They should get someone to make a cover for this entrance.

A couple of people were talking in the hold. It was too dark to see who they were, but one of the voices was Nellie's.

"No, you can't see him." She sounded distressed. "My mistress has told me that no one can talk to him unless she is there—oh! Mistress Johanna, there you are."

The people who were with Nellie at the bottom of the stairs looked up and by the grey light from the rainy day, Johanna recognised their faces: Johan Delacoeur and Fleuris LaFontaine. What were they doing here?

"Good morning, gentlemen," she said, while climbing down. She made sure that her annoyance came through in her tone, which wasn't hard when she was wet and cold and desperate to get changed into dry clothes.

Since when did citizens encroach on the King's freedom? She had told Nellie that she wanted no visitors here, which was Roald's domain, where he was safe from prying eyes. The guards would know that, too. They should have stopped the men.

Roald sat at his desk, studiously ignoring the nobles, but the way in which he jiggled his leg showed that he was already pretty distressed, even though outsiders wouldn't pick up on it.

Johanna had arrived at the bottom of the stairs and now faced the men, both of whom were much taller than her. "Do you have a pressing reason to bother the king in his private quarters?"

"The matter is quite urgent." Johan Delacoeur's manner was so distant that he didn't even look into her eyes.

"Ah, I see. You have come here to discuss the details of the coronation ceremony that we must hold soon."

"Um . . ." They clearly had not.

"Well, come down, and we'll discuss it."

"Miss Brouwer," began Fleuris LaFontaine, and that was not a good beginning at all.

"Why the 'Miss'? Am I not your queen?"

"That's what we're here to talk about."

"I don't understand." Her heart thudded in her chest. Why discuss this now? They'd had two months to question her status. What had changed?

"None of us witnessed the ceremony that you say took place on the deck of this ship near the ruins of Aroden castle. The only witness appears to be the maid who performed the ceremony and a demon-possessed witch. We cannot verify the young maid's claim that she is authorised to conduct such a ceremony—"

"Well then, it's easy, we must hold the wedding ceremony again. As long as it's organised quickly, because it would look improper if I attended it looking like I swallowed a water bag."

It was all bluff, but Fleuris gave her an uncertain look. "But certainly it's a bit early to . . . Are you certain? We cannot hold the ceremony then, in your condition . . ."

"It's early days yet. We have time. But if you would like to see an official ceremony, then we must hold one." A chill came over her. Would they really cast out a woman who carried the king's first-born? Would they cast out any woman in that condition, knowing that she would have nowhere else to go?

Johan Delacoeur was looking at her with an *I-don't-believe-this* expression on his face. "I would like to see a ruling from a physic before we make any rash decisions."

"I have been with Roald since we fled Saardam. I saved him. I helped him all that time." *I dressed him, I fed him.* "There is nothing 'rash' about this decision."

"Yes, but I think it would be more appropriate for the new king to be wed to a girl from a good family."

"I am not one of your approved candidates, is that it? Can I mention that at the ball on the night before the fire, all of the approved candidates danced with him, and most of the girls thumbed their noses at 'the idiot prince'? Some even ran back to their mothers crying. They would not have fished him out of the harbour. They would not have put up with his strange comments."

Neither of the men she faced had unmarried daughters of the right age anyway, and the problem had been deeper than that: the king had fallen out with the Council of Nobles over the king's encouragement of the Church of the Triune.

And she realised something even more terrible: maybe Roald was *meant* to have died in the fire or drowned in the harbour. She had assumed that he had jumped in the water to escape fire and that, being a strong swimmer, he'd judged the water a safe escape. Could it be that someone had pushed him? Maybe this was all part of a plot to get rid of not only the Church of the Triune, but its most vocal supporter. Maybe they had wanted to replace Nicholaos with one of the king's Burovian cousins.

Heart thudding, she looked into the old and haughty faces of the two men opposite her. They *appeared* quite civilised, but especially with nobles, appearances never told the entire story.

"Why don't you ask the king what *he* wants."

Johan Delacoeur scoffed. "He's not in a state to—"

"He is *not* dumb if that's what you were going to say."

"No, I wasn't."

Yes, that was exactly what he was going to say. "Roald?"

He sat bent over his book, but his eyes weren't moving. He held his hands clamped between his knees, and a muscle in his forearm kept alternately tensing up and relaxing.

"Roald?" She put an arm over his shoulder. Drops of sweat pearled on his forehead. He smelled sweaty, too.

"I was rude to them," he said.

Fleuris LaFontaine snorted. "He was, too. I don't know where a prince learns that kind of language."

"They were rude to *my* women," Roald said. "The maid and the witch. No one is rude to *my* women."

"I know. It's all right." She spoke very softly, hoping that the men couldn't hear her well enough to understand.

"You're mine. Nellie is mine. They can't be rude to you."

"It's all right, really. Calm down, please."

"Your Majesty," said Fleuris LaFontaine.

"Tell them to leave," Roald said.

"They won't listen to me. You're the king. Tell them."

"I can't talk to them. They're rude. Father says I can't talk to rude people."

Johan Delacoeur cleared his throat. "Your Majesty . . ."

Johanna turned around. Why couldn't he see that she was busy? "The king will talk to you if he wants. Right now, he asks me to tell you to leave."

Johan ignored her. "Please do tell us, Your Majesty, if you would prefer to wed a woman of your status—"

Roald got up from the table so suddenly that Johanna had no chance to stop him. He faced the two men.

"They are *my* women! You can't take them away from me. I forbid you to take them away from me. I'm the king, you have to listen to me and do what I say. I want you to leave. This is my room for me and my women."

"Roald, it's all right. Calm down."

"No, it's not all right. They are here to take you away. I don't want you to go. You're mine. I love you." His cheeks had gone red.

"Roald . . ."

He turned back to the men, whose eyes were wide. Johan Delacoeur's mouth hung open.

"You hear that? I love her. Now, you leave. Get out of here. This is *my* ship. Go, go, go." He more or less pushed them up the stairs, Johan Delacoeur first and then his colleague.

Fleuris LaFontaine stammered, "Your Majesty, I'm sorry to have caused offense. It was not my intention—"

"Go, go, go!" Roald was almost shrieking now.

"Come, my friend," Johan said from the top of the stairs. "We know we're not wanted." He met Johanna's eyes. "I can only say, young lady, that this is a very bad move—"

"Go, go, go! Stop talking. Stop making noise. Yap, yap, yap, yap. Get out of here."

Fleuris LaFontaine had reached the top of the stairs, his face red from exertion. Men of his standing did apparently *not* run up narrow and steep stairs.

They pushed the cover shut, and Johanna was left alone with Roald.

They looked at each other.

Johanna stifled a snort of laughter.

"You think that's funny?"

"I think you were brilliant." There would be consequences, but the sight of those two portly men scrambling up the steps was not one she'd forget quickly.

"You liked it." He said that in a tone as if he could barely believe it.

"Yes, I did."

He started laughing, too. "Did you see how scared they were? How I chased them up the stairs?"

Johanna laughed out loud. She put on an arrogant voice. "Your Majesty, wouldn't you prefer to wed a woman of your status?"

Roald giggled and snorted.

"They could hardly be more crass about what they wanted. And you know what the funny thing is? Ha, ha, ha. They don't even have any daughters."

Roald squealed with laughter.

Nellie poked her head in. "Well, I'm glad you're having fun. Those men were *most* rude."

Johanna was laughing too much to reply.

"Well, I'm getting dinner ready," Nellie said, and closed the cover to the hold.

Poor Nellie. When was the last time she'd laughed?

Johanna let herself fall on the bed and Roald dropped next to her. She heaved a satisfied sigh, staring at the rough underside of the hold cover.

Then wriggled an elbow under her so that she could look at Roald.

"You're all wet."

"Yes, the weather outside is horrible."

His eyes were fixed on her. The light from the lamp fell sideways on his face. His beard had gotten a lot denser, which made him look more like a king every day. She stroked the rough hair. There were blond hairs and darker ones and fox-red ones.

She whispered, "I love you."

"No, you got that wrong. I should say that to you."

"Yes, but I love you, too." And strange as it sounded, it was the truth.

He frowned. "No one has ever said that to me."

"Not even your mother?"

He shook his head. "You really love me?"

"Yes."

His expression was so shocked that it made her all weepy. "Come on, Roald, you're making me cry."

"You can't cry. I'm supposed to make you happy."

"You do make me happy. They're happy tears." She kissed him softly on the lips.

From one thing came another, and when Nellie came a bit later to say that dinner was ready, Johanna and Roald weren't quite ready for dinner.

CHAPTER 9

I N THE NEXT few days, it rained a lot more. The river broke its banks on the eastern side as well as the western side and started encroaching on the camp. Some people in the lower parts of the meadow had to move their tents, which made the higher side of the meadow very crowded.

With the help of Captain Arense, Johanna found two young men who agreed to be scouts and check on the situation in Saardam. Master Deim helped organise a small dinghy, and Johanna leant them a harness and two placid sea cows so that they could come back again.

Johanna watched them go with a pang of apprehension. The river was an expanse of churning, muddy water and the men had to harness the animals just to be able to control the little boat. If they were hit by a floating tree trunk, they would have no chance. But both men assured her that they could swim and she knew both of them had experience with boats. Still, who knew what they'd meet in Saardam?

Johanna attended one more Council of Nobles meeting

where she proposed that to cheer up the people, there would an official wedding ceremony at a date to be announced soon.

The nobles didn't like it, but there was nothing they could do when Master Deim, Joris DeCamp and Captain Arense all supported the idea. She sure hadn't seen the end of their protests, but for now the nobles were outmanoeuvred.

A few days later, Johanna was in the camp talking to some of the women about things the refugees collectively needed to barter in town, like better clothing for the wet weather, shoes, and a cart and horse. A young lad came rushing in to tell her that a man in the Baron's red livery had gone to the *Lady Sara*. Johanna's first thought was: news from Saardam. She hurried back, sidestepping puddles and areas of mud. By the time she came to the jetty, the man was just coming down the gangplank. He nodded to her when meeting her coming the other way. Wet and bedraggled as she was, he probably thought she was a maid.

Roald sat staring at a piece of parchment on his desk.

Her heart jumped. Bad news? Please, no. "What is it?"

He said nothing, so she looked over his shoulder. No, it was not from Saardam. The letter bore the Red Baron's family seal. In elegant, curly script it said,

It has come to my attention that Your Royal Majesty and the consort are planning to hold an official ceremony to celebrate your holy matrimony. We simply cannot allow for a ceremony of import to be held in a cow paddock. We offer the use of our grand hall in the castle for this purpose. Please send your personal servants around to talk about the arrangements.

The letter was signed Baroness Viktoriya, whose name she had never heard, but who had only been referred to as "The Baroness" whenever people spoke of her.

Johanna frowned. They hadn't even set a date yet, and nothing about this wedding was official. If nothing else, this confirmed that someone in the camp was close to the Baron, even if the Baron seemed to avoid her and the nobles of the council.

"I don't understand," Roald said. "We can't get married. We are already married."

"I know, but the nobles want another ceremony because they couldn't be at the first one."

"Oh." Roald said, and he frowned. "Why? I don't like ceremonies. I don't want another ball."

"If I have anything to do with it, there won't be another ball." But if the Baron's family insisted on having the ceremony at the castle, there would be a ball with lots of unfamiliar important noble people.

Worse, she couldn't see a polite way to refuse the offer.

Worse still, Kylian would be there.

And the letter absolutely needed replying to, so Johanna wrote a polite reply that she'd be delighted to visit the next day, but she had to force herself to write that word *delighted*. Who in the camp had told the Baroness this?

Johanna wasn't going to let Nellie go to the castle by herself, so she decided to go with Nellie and two guards the next morning. Both Johanna and Nellie got dressed in their best outfits, which still left a lot to be desired. Nellie was nervous, wanting to know if it was really necessary for her to come, because she was only a maid.

"A lady-in-waiting," Johanna corrected, "and you absolutely should come, because I can trust you."

Nellie looked nothing like a maid in the old-fashioned dress they had taken from Duke Lothar's castle. The dark colour of the fabric made her skin look pale and ghost-like. Johanna promised herself that as soon as they were out of this camp, she would get Nellie some proper clothes that did not make her look like a walking corpse.

Fortunately, the rain had let up a bit, even though the streets in the town were still muddy. The townsfolk wore raincoats of oiled cloth and tall boots. Some children played barefoot in the mud. A couple of foreign guests doing their best to avoid puddles in their best clothes drew a certain amount of attention.

At the castle, they walked across the heavy drawbridge and announced themselves at the gate, where a guard told them to come with him to meet the Baroness. From inside, the castle looked as austere and plain as it did from the outside. Walls were made from bare stone, and mostly unadorned. Passages were high-ceilinged and empty. Any furniture was made from heavy oak, stained dark. Dark and menacing suits of armour lined the corridors where their footsteps echoed hollow. What little light fell through the windows looked washed out and wan.

"It's creepy in here," Nellie said in a low voice, glancing over her shoulder. "As if those suits of armour are going to come to life and jump on us when we're not looking."

The guard led them into a huge but very dark hall, where many long tables and benches stood in rows. Johanna could imagine wedding guests seated at those tables, laughing and eating. The air smelled of stale beer mixed with a faint waft of roast meat.

A couple of dark wooden chandeliers hung from the ceiling, but none of the candles burned. Johanna's first thought was that the hall had nothing like the splendour of the gorgeous ballroom in the palace in Saardam. But it was a hundred times better than holding the ceremony in the muddy field of the camp, which might well be half-submerged if this rain kept up.

Still, she did not want to accept any more of the Baron's charity.

This whole idea of having a wedding was silly. It would be much better to have it when they were back in Saardam.

But the nobles would see that she'd lied about being

with child.

The sound of a clear female voice disturbed her thoughts. The woman who walked towards her between the tables had the figure of a matron: broad-hipped and large-breasted, with her greying hair piled on top of her head in a bun, held in place by a jewelled net. Her dress was made from thick velvet in the darkest of red.

"You are the princess Johanna, right?" She spoke with a heavy and very unusual accent.

"I am. It's an honour to meet you. Thank you for your hospitality."

The Baroness waved her be-ringed hand. "Oh, it is nothing. I'm so excited to host a wedding. My son, he will not get married. I tell him about which girls is looking to marry. Nice girls. Rich girls, but he just say nothing. Every time I ask him, he change subject."

Her accent was really unusual, as were her dark brown eyes.

"Is a pity that you're already married. I say to him: what is happening to castle and land when your father dies? But he just laugh. Now we receive letters from Aroden, from Burovia, even from Lurezia. The parents tell us: 'At his last visit, your son was besotted with our daughter. I think it might be beneficial to let them marry.' Oh . . ." She spread her hands and looked at the ceiling. "By the Holy Spirit, we get one at least every month. Rich men's daughters, princesses even! My son, he is a nice, decent young man. He does not go break the hearts of all these girls."

She sighed and shook her head in a *what-has-the-world-come-to* kind of way. Johanna thought of Kylian's attempts to seduce her, and decided not to pierce the Baroness' bubble of delusion about her son's decency.

The Baroness talked and talked and talked. She had the whole thing planned out already. What Johanna would wear, what Roald would wear, where they would sit, which dances would be played, the guest list, and so forth and so on.

Johanna could make use of the kitchens, she said, as well as the courtiers. It would be a joint festivity for the Saarlander refugees and the esteemed citizens of Florisheim.

Johanna had been afraid of that.

But her carefully-worded suggestion to invite mainly people from Saardam "to keep costs down" was swept aside with, "Oh, but don't worry about the money. It will all be on our account. We *love* a good feast. It's at harvest time, so we will have plenty." And, "Don't worry that you don't know many people. I will personally introduce you to citizens of Florisheim. They will be delighted to meet you."

Johanna gnashed her teeth in frustration. She didn't *want* to be introduced to all the citizens of Florisheim. Maybe some other time she would, but right now, she just wanted to go home.

The Baroness' plans were like a spider's web: once you were stuck, you could not get free, no matter how much you tried. The Baroness herself sat like a big fat spider in the middle of the web. Sickly sweet, dressed up like a favourite auntie, but impossible to escape from.

Was there such thing as magic through words?

Not to mention that the Baron's feasts were fertile ground for feuds and poisonings, and she wanted nothing more than to get out of that dark room. She glanced at Nellie, who hadn't been able to get a word in at all, and who looked as desperate to leave as Johanna felt.

She didn't want to hold the ceremony in the Baron's castle. She didn't want the nobles of Florisheim to be there, because not only did she know none of them, but she would have no idea if any of them would be there for other reasons. The Baron would probably be there, as well as his son who she was trying to avoid.

Yet she knew she couldn't politely refuse this offer.

Worse, this woman just kept on talking.

Finally, Johanna managed to cut off the visit by politely refusing tea "because I have to be back to help my husband with the midday meal." It was only a half-lie. Roald would happily eat by himself—just the applesauce, and he'd leave the rest—but it finally did the trick. After asking Johanna about her earlier unofficial wedding, and announcing, "We can't have a king be married in old farmer's clothes and dirty jacket," Johanna and Nellie were finally allowed to go. The same guard who had brought them in—and who had been waiting patiently by the door—accompanied them to the gate.

Johanna kept her silence until they were safely in the market square.

"Why in all of the heaven's name does that woman think she owns me?"

Nellie frowned at her. "What do you mean? I don't understand. She is just being friendly and helping us. We can hardly hold the wedding in a muddy field."

Not you, too. "Nellie, she has no reason for doing this. We are not her relatives. If I'm correct, she comes from the east, the land of wolves. She has no connection to Saardam—"

"Does she have to have a connection to us? Why can't she just help us? Why do you always expect the worst of people?"

Johanna spread her hands. *Because people try the worst on me when they think I'm not looking?* But that argument was lost on Nellie. One day, someone would betray poor Nellie so badly, it would break her heart, and then would she still find it in her to forgive this person? Yes, she probably would.

Nellie's tendency to trust everyone had always infuriated

her as much as Johanna's tendency to distrust people had infuriated Nellie. It really could not be helped. It was engrained in Nellie's character.

And there was nothing she could do to refuse the Baroness' hospitality, even though the thought of having to see that woman again made her skin crawl. She did not want to be ensnared in this web of stickiness masquerading as hospitality. She did not want to see Kylian. But for now, she could see no escape.

She asked Nellie how much she wanted to be involved in the wedding preparations, which was quite a bit, but she said, "I'll need a lot of help, mistress."

So later that day, Johanna set about getting that help. Mistress Daphne or any of the modistes from Saardam had been below Fleuris LaFontaine's status to offer them a place on the *Prosperity*, but some of the noble women knew about fashion, and a lot of them complained bitterly of having too little to do. She went in search of Julianna Nieland, who lived in one of the tents with a distant uncle of hers and whom she hadn't seen much since coming to the camp.

Johanna announced herself at the door.

"Wait, I'll get her for you," said the young man who came to see what she wanted.

He made a small bow, and Johanna could see the loyalty to the royal family written on his face.

A moment later, another man pushed aside the tent flap. He was older, dressed in a velvet coat and riding pants. Julianna's uncle was a horseman, she remembered. He gave her a suspicious look before bowing stiffly and turning back inside.

"Don't make too much useless women's gossip," he said inside the tent.

"I'm all right, uncle," Julianna replied. "I won't bother you." And she finally came to the entrance.

Julianna had always had a full figure that Johanna secretly

admired, but the young woman in drab clothing who shuffled into view was as thin as a skeleton.

"I've been unwell," she said in response to Johanna's shocked look.

Unwell and unwelcome, if her uncle's strange behaviour was anything to go by.

Now she felt sorry for not having checked up on Julianna earlier. "I need some women to come and help me with the wedding. I thought you might like to do that." She had to do her best not to cringe.

Julianna put her finger to her lips and pulled Johanna away from the tent. Her grip was both strong and seeking support in holding herself up. Johanna put her arm around Julianna's shoulder, feeling Julianna's bones through her clothing.

"I've been really sick. Ate something bad and couldn't keep anything down for days."

"I heard that it was going through the camp." Several people had been very ill. "I hope your family are all right."

"They are. My uncle says I'm blaming my aunt for bad cooking, even though I never said so and I would never say anything as ungrateful as that. He says I was faking illness, but I wouldn't even know how to fake something like this. Please, let me do something for you, because these people drive me crazy."

"Then come to the *Lady Sara* every day to help Nellie and Loesie sew. A couple of good servings of Nellie's food will sort you out."

So Julianna came to the sitting room in the *Lady Sara*'s hold. She had trouble with the stairs, and Johanna worried about what "I've been unwell" really meant. Clearly a lot more than just a simple illness for a couple of days. Nellie brought cakes and biscuits, but Julianna ate only half a biscuit.

To Johanna's plans for an official wedding, she made an

effort to show enthusiasm, but the tone of her voice wasn't convincing. Moreover, she didn't like Julianna's coughing, big, heavy wet coughs.

"Please, Julianna, let me help you. If you want a medic to come, I have the name of a herb woman who is supposed to be really good."

"It's all right. I'm a lot better already." She illustrated this with a coughing fit.

If that was "a lot better", Johanna didn't want to know about worse parts. "You must come here every day, and I'll make sure that you eat enough. You have to get well again."

Julianna looked down at the thin hands she held clenched in her lap. "What does it matter? All my family are dead anyway."

"You don't know that."

"I saw my house burn. No one can survive a fire like that. No one of my parents' age anyway."

"Octavio was at the ball. You were there with him." She remembered how he'd been condescending to her while begging Father for her hand. Octavio Nieland was good friends with Ignatius Hemeldinck, she remembered.

Julianna's face tightened. "It's Father and Mother I worry about. They're not young."

"I am really sorry. I'm pretty much in the same situation. I don't know where Father is. I have no idea if he's still alive."

Julianna shook her head. "You're not in the same situation. You got out during the fire. You weren't there for what happened after the fire. Octavio . . ." She clamped her hands between her knees and shuddered visibly.

"What happened to Octavio? I saw him outside the palace that night."

"He doesn't really care about me or about any of us. He only cares about power. I should have realised that long ago. You know I used to think that he was stupid about wanting to marry you, because you weren't from a noble family?" She looked down. "Well, I'm sorry about that. I was really stupid. I didn't see that it was all about the Brouwer Company, which he wanted. I just didn't want to see how important money was for him."

Johanna's heart jumped. "*Was?* Did something happen to him?"

A tear glistened in Julianna's eye. "Something happened all right. He joined Alexandre Trebuchet. Apparently, they knew each other from when Octavio lodged with Mother's cousin in Lurezia and they were friends there."

"You *met* that man? What is he like?"

Julianna shrugged. "Just another young man. He's got a sharp face and dark brown hair, which he wears in a ponytail, not unlike my brother. He keeps saying how he saved Saardam and how good he is."

"Saved? What from?"

"Isn't it obvious? That church that got all of the king's money. I guess it's all irrelevant now, but they were not bad people. They didn't deserve to be killed in the street, to have their houses burnt and possessions stolen."

"Just the church people?" Johanna thought of several church families she knew—Nellie's family and Master Willems—and wondered if any of them had been victims. "When you saw Alexandre, did you see any evidence of magic?"

Julianna gave her a *what-do-you-take-me-for* look. "He has bands of rogues helping him silence people who disagreed with him. There were men with bears and other animals. One of them had a big cat with spots. They went around all the houses and dragged everyone out. If they didn't like you, they burned your house."

Johanna had heard a bit about those days. Apparently the survivors had been taken to the town hall, which had survived the fire, as had many stone buildings surrounding the market place. In the town hall, Alexandre had addressed them in a long and rambling speech mostly incomprehensible for people unfamiliar with Burovian.

Several people in the camp had spoken of Alexandre's orders to hand over any remaining church supporters or face death. The Saarlanders had been asked to betray their fellow kinsfolk, the people they had grown up with, their neighbours. Some people in the camp, especially the women, had spoken of how appalled they were. They were glad, they said, that the young Shepherd Carolus had made it onto the ship, even though no one was sure how he had managed that, presumably because he was mostly still known in town under his given name of Dirk Goedthart and he had been well-known in town as a well-off merchant's son until he joined the church and went to the seminary.

"If only Father had been there. He would have told Octavio exactly what he thought." Julianna's eyes brimmed with tears. Johanna didn't know what it was like to have a brother, but she imagined not having a brother was better than having a brother who betrayed his town like this.

Julianna launched into another coughing fit.

Poor Julianna. Johanna told her to be careful and get plenty of fresh air. After making Julianna promise that she'd be back the next day, Johanna watched her climb up the stairs with all the mobility of a woman of eighty.

Johanna had to go up and close the hold door, because Julianna wasn't strong enough to do it. Rain still fell, so she went back down into the sitting room.

It was a sign of Roald's condition that he had continued to sit and read through all this, and had completely ignored any mention of his name.

Johanna dropped onto the bed and lay staring at the

rough and dusty undersides of the hold covers for a while, but staring wasn't going to get anything done.

She pushed herself up and went to Roald.

"I am going to need your help." She put an arm over his shoulder.

He continued reading.

"Roald?"

He glanced at her. "This book is interesting. It says that if you keep sailing a boat around the Horn, you will find a whole other world like ours. I wonder if people live there."

"They do. That's where the eastern traders are from."

"Yes, everyone talks about them, but has anyone seen these people?"

"Some have." She believed Father and Master Deim had, or at least some of the seafaring captains.

"Then why do books like these contain no diagrams of what they look like?" He held up the book. The front cover said, *On the Travels of the Known Lands*.

"I'm not sure."

"Are they dangerous?"

"I don't know." Father talked about the eastern traders a lot, because they brought the spices that he sold. He told her that they were smart people who sailed on big square-looking ships with red sails. The ships were big enough for the men to take their entire families. Many of them lived at sea and didn't go home after each voyage. They were nimble and independent, unlike the seafaring captains of Saardam, who returned with their wares to sell, to pay their investors and to rustle the next lot of investors to outfit their next trip.

Some people suggested that the eastern traders could become dangerous if given too much freedom to sail along the coast, but she didn't want to go into that discussion now. She put her hand over the book. "Roald, look at me. I need your help."

"Oh?" His expression was startled.

"We need to hold an official wedding as soon as possible."

"But we're already married."

"I know that, but the people in the camp won't accept it until we hold the ceremony before their eyes." She now understood how much stress ceremonies placed on him and it pained her to ask him to be present at another one. "We also need to hold an official coronation ceremony."

"Oh." He gave her a blank look. "Do I have to do anything for that?"

You're the king, for crying out loud! "I want you to write a proclamation. We'll set a date and make a formal announcement."

"Oh." He looked confused. "Can't you do those things for me?"

"They won't listen to me unless we're officially married in their eyes."

"Oh."

"That's why I need you to write a proclamation that we will hold a wedding. They can all see that it's official."

"All right." And after a brief silence, he added, "She suffers from bad air."

"What on Earth are you talking about?"

"The woman who was just here. She suffers from bad air. Many people in the camp have it. It's from the cold and damp and having many people sleeping cramped together in tents."

There wasn't much that Johanna could do about that other than try to get out of this camp as soon as possible. This was summer. Conditions would get much worse in winter. People said that, in these parts, snow fell almost every year.

There was no way they could stay here for winter. She decided for herself that she would take the *Lady Sara* with whomever it could carry back to Saardam after the wedding, at the very latest.

How she would do it, she didn't know, but the people would not spend winter in this cold and damp field.

More importantly, she would not stay here where Roald had little support and where either of them might get sick at any time.

Most importantly of all, she would not stay because her bleeding was late.

Johanna helped Roald write a declaration. He took a long time, but his handwriting was beautiful and he signed it with a loopy signature. Master Deim put the parchment up on the wall of the boat shed that was fast becoming the equivalent of the mayor's house. The wedding ceremony would be held on the first of the month of October. Johanna hoped that she would show the signs of being with child by then.

She went to see the Shepherd Carolus, who announced that he'd be "most delighted" to conduct the ceremony and then looked at her with misty eyes. He had a youthful face, with freckles on his cheeks and playful blond curls of hair that, no matter how much he smoothed them down, always found a way to stand up.

"Shepherd Romulus would have loved to do this," he said in a voice filled with emotion.

Johanna nodded, silently.

"They killed him. They burned the church. They stole all the clothes and food we kept stored for winter to give to people in need. Why? I don't understand."

Johanna put a hand on his shoulder. "We will go back. We will rebuild. They can try to wipe us out, but they can't kill us."

A few days later, the Baroness Viktoriya heard about the wedding date, and announced that the grand hall would be at their disposal. Johanna reluctantly agreed to hold the ceremony there, much to the approval of the nobles.

Julianna came faithfully every day. She sat at the table in the hold and ate whatever Nellie brought. At first, Johanna had to force her, but after two days, her appetite started returning with her chattiness, which made Johanna remember why she had never liked Julianna much. Rather than get annoyed at it—a major achievement—Johanna asked Julianna to casually chat to people in the camp and listen to what they said. Julianna took to her task with enthusiasm and reported back every day.

"Everyone wants to go back to their houses," she said.

"Why do they think we're not returning?"

"Because the council says it's too dangerous. Alexandre is a strong magician. They are afraid because they have never dealt much with magic before. Some are happy to wait, but some are saying that magic or no, we should go back and drive him out. Some of the young men are prepared to fight."

Julianna mentioned a list of names, most of whom were merchants or nobles who weren't involved with the ones who made decisions in the council.

Then she worried about the two scouts she had sent. They should have been back by now, although it might be taking them longer because of the high water.

Unfortunately, Julianna said that she had been unable to dig up further information about what kind of deal with the Baron was keeping the nobles in Florisheim. But Johanna had heard some rumours while listening to the older children tag behind Roald in his frog-hunting.

A boy had said, "My father says that we can't go back until the whole of Saardam has been cleaned up, and he says Alexandre just wants to do a good job."

To which a younger boy had said, "Well, *my* father says that your father is crazy."

After which they started an *is-not—is-so—is-not* word fight, which only stopped when someone in the reeds shouted for them to be quiet. "You're scaring the frogs!"

And with the wet weather frogs were, unfortunately, everywhere.

But that little snatch of conversation got Johanna's thoughts off to an uncomfortable tangent. Because what if the nobles had *asked* Alexandre to drive out the church, and now Alexandre, and his friend the Baron, would no longer speak to the men?

Johanna and Julianna stood on the deck of the *Lady Sara*, overlooking the camp. The rain had eased somewhat and the water level had dropped a little bit.

"There are lots of young men in the camp who want to return and fight," Julianna said.

"There is little point in fighting magic with arms," Johanna said. "We need to fight magic with magic."

"But we don't have magic."

"That's why we must find a court magician."

And that meant making deals with possibly unpleasant people. Out of all the magicians she knew, Duke Lothar and Sylvan were the ones she trusted most, but she doubted they'd help her. By association, she *should* have more trust in Kylian than she did, but as yet she didn't understand all the different sides to the assassination attempt by the Duke of his half-brother Baron Uti. The strange thing was that many of the locals seemed to consider this attempt a great source of hilarity. Johanna struggled to make sense of the relationships of the Baron and his family. If Kylian was welcome at Duke Lothar's castle, did that mean that he supported the attempt to kill his father?

She had considered asking the duke to help her, but he

and his son were pretty much unreachable from here. She'd asked couriers to take a letter to him, but they all refused to go into the forest.

Probably because people go missing in those woods. And ended up in that ice cellar.

Johanna desperately didn't want to get involved in the case of the ice cellar. But she needed a magician.

"We also need ships," Johanna said, pushing away uncomfortable thoughts about magic and having to rely on people she didn't trust. "I've got the *Lady Sara*, but that's not enough for everyone."

She looked up the river, still swollen from the recent rain. From here to Saardam was all downstream. They didn't need animals, although they would take them regardless, and getting to Saardam from here would probably take less than a day on the strong current.

"We can have the *Prosperity*," Julianna said. "Captain Arense supports us and the ship can carry many people."

"We're going back as soon as we can," Johanna said. "Don't tell anyone, just try to gauge who would come if we gave them the word." If she had sorted the magician problem.

"When?"

"As soon as possible after the wedding." Maybe even before. Maybe she needed to keep up the illusion that there was to be a wedding and that nothing would happen before that time, in order not to raise suspicion from the nobles or the Baron, or anyone else. Because the more she thought about it, the more she was convinced that she didn't want to hold her wedding in that gloomy castle, attended by the Baron's guests and family: Baroness Viktoriya the fat spider in her web, and Kylian the Necromancer.

The next morning, she woke up to find her nightshirt drenched with blood.

CHAPTER 10

THE BLEEDING came with strong cramps, and Johanna stayed in the cabin for a day. Master Deim and Julianna came to see her because they were worried. At their subtle hints that she was with child, she could only laugh. If only. She didn't understand why this happened. She *thought* they did everything right.

Loesie was not helpful when she said, "Didn't happen for Annette's ma until she'd been married three years. Never happened to her since. They got Annette, which must have been a mistake, because she was much too pretty for the farm."

Annette was Loesie's neighbour. Loesie's mother, of course, had been with child after a dalliance with a foreign visitor.

There *were* women who never had children, but Johanna was determined not to have that happen to her.

"I'm going into town," she said to Nellie the next morning.

"Do you want me to come, mistress Johanna?" She and

Loesie were peeling and cutting apples for the applesauce that Roald liked so much.

"It might be a good idea, but I'm visiting a herb woman who is said to have magic, so it might be better if Loesie came."

Loesie gave her a sharp look. "Don't want to have anything to do with magic. Nothing good ever came from it."

"We're just going to visit this woman. You don't need to say anything. I want you there because you are the only one who could tell if she's using magic. And I also want you to see what the wood says about who visited the house and what was said in any of the rooms, wherever we get the chance."

Loesie grumbled. "There is never anything 'just' about magic."

"I'm going to ask her for herbs."

Loesie gave her a suspicious look. Seen from this angle, her father's foreign blood became obvious. People in eastern Estland, Gelre and Burovia tended to be darker and taller than the Saarlanders. Loesie was not soft, friendly and feminine. She was lanky and all angles with deep-set, intense eyes. "We can just as well ask for herbs at the markets."

"This woman is supposed to be very good."

"This is not still about the bleeding, right?"

Nellie cut in, about to start peeling another apple. "Loesie, it is really important that the mistress has a child soon."

"Bah, children are annoying and too much trouble." Loesie threw a hand full of apple pieces in the pan and took off her apron. "But I'll come, because if I don't, she will get us into even more trouble." She went into the cabin.

Nellie's gaze followed her, and her mouth twitched. Not happy, clearly. Maybe she considered it her duty to come with Johanna.

Johanna said, "Do keep an eye on Roald so that he doesn't go wandering off too far."

"Yes, mistress. Certainly." Still not happy by the tone of her voice.

Come to think of it, Nellie had been pretty unhappy the last few days, and Johanna couldn't quite work out why. Compared to when they were with the bandits, the ship was comfortable, and Nellie even had her own bed. There was enough to eat and Nellie's status had vastly improved.

She would worry about her family, but then again, everyone did.

Not too much later, Johanna and Loesie walked down the rickety jetty to the riverbank. The water level had fallen a bit, but the water was still only an arm's length under the walkway.

The guards who stood there gave friendly nods, but didn't ask if they should come. Roald was still on board, and they didn't care about her.

Johanna and Loesie walked quickly along the path. Because it was so wet, people had made tracks through the tall grass higher on the riverbank to avoid muddy areas. Those tracks were narrow and they had to walk behind each other. The weather was muggy, and building clouds on the horizon heralded more thunderstorms. Would the rains ever stop?

The track joined the main road in the curve of the river, and when she could finally walk next to Loesie, Johanna wasn't sure what to say. Loesie had been distant since the demon had been driven out of her, saying about the incident only that she "didn't remember much", but never quite meeting Johanna's eyes when she said this.

Her attempts to deny magic and turn into an obedient domestic maid would be funny if Johanna didn't expect that there was a more sinister reason behind them, and she had no idea how to find out what that reason was.

"I'm going to need your help, Loesie," she said after a long and uncomfortable silence.

"I'm already helping."

"Yes, and thank you for that. I love your lace. It's really pretty." They walked another distance before she added, "But it's help of a different kind I'll need."

Loesie raised her eyebrows.

"Alexandre Trebuchet who rules Saardam is a fire magician. People from the camp want to go back there and drive him out. Some of them are offering to fight, but we can't get rid of Alexandre with an army. We need magicians. My magic is weak and insignificant. You are the only other person in the camp with any magic. I would like you to go to the Magician's Guild here in Florisheim to receive training so that you can be our court magician."

"Didn't I tell you that nothing good ever comes from magic?"

"You did, but in this case the bad things have already happened. We need to fix them."

"You don't understand at all."

"Then explain it to me so that I can help you."

"I do not want to be helped. We should not be using magic."

"But Alexandre is using magic! We have no hope of defeating him with an army, no matter how many men we get and how good they are." Johanna tried to push down her frustration. Getting angry wouldn't achieve anything. "At least tell me why."

Loesie pressed her mouth into a thin line. Her gaze shifted to somewhere over Johanna's shoulder on the opposite riverbank. Johanna turned to look, but saw nothing that caught her attention.

"Please, Loesie. I don't want to hire a foreign magician

and I will have to if you don't do it. We don't know who we can trust."

"You don't want to go hiring magicians at all."

"No, I don't." At least they could agree on that.

"Not me, and no one else." Loesie met Johanna's eyes with that intense look. She let a long silence lapse. Johanna thought she wasn't going to say anything, but then she added, "Someone or *something* has messed with the magic lines. I can feel it in my bones, and everyone who's got more magic than me would feel it even more."

"Duke Lothar was talking about magic lines, right?" She thought of the tunnels made from tortured trees and then remembered that Loesie would not have seen them because she'd still been possessed. Johanna had felt no desire to visit that place after the exorcism was done, and Loesie would not have had the strength to do so had she wished to see it.

"Magic lines are everywhere. There is a strong one under most of the Saar River. Sometimes the willows grow so stunted that you can't even find branches to cut for making baskets. The horses that try to swim across the river grow webbed feet and they turn into water horses. And the grazing cows get so mad from eating the grass that they dance through the meadow."

Johanna nodded, a shiver running over her back. She had seen cows do that, especially in spring when they first came outside. Horses, too, although she wasn't too sure about the webbed feet.

"All those magic lines join up and split again, like a giant . . . fishing net under the ground. Sometimes they come to the surface. That's where you get trouble. Like across the river from my granpa's farm . . . ." For a moment her eyes misted over. "Like the ghosts, and the funny trees and water horses, and all the evil magics, like bear magic."

"Necromancers?"

Loesie nodded, clamping her arms around herself. "That's what the rumour says anyway. I think ghosts happen because people die while having unfinished business, I don't think magicians have anything to do with it. But by us using the magic, more of the lines come up, like a tailor unravelling a thread. Once a thread is up, you can't put it back into the ground. We shouldn't be using magic."

"That's all very well for you to say, but should we just sit like ducks and let magicians rule us and kill all of us? Shouldn't we learn about magic so that we can defend ourselves, or just save ourselves?"

That earned her another suspicious look.

"Loesie, please. I have no one else that I can trust."

"I won't do it, and you shouldn't be trusting me anyway. You're a nice, pretty, innocent girl, like Annette. She's dead now, and it's my fault. I'll do your washing and your sewing until you have better people to do it. But do not ask me to do magic for you, because you have no idea what you're asking."

"I'm not innocent."

"Yes, you are."

"Then why won't you tell me what is going on? Why did you even wait so long to tell me this?" She spread her hands in frustration.

Loesie whirled around. "Because I don't want you to die as well!" Her eyes were wild and there was more colour in her cheeks than Johanna had ever seen. "And you deserve better than that. Annette deserved better. It all happened because of me, and because of evil magic. I don't know how many times I have to say this: if you want herbs, buy herbs. Don't meddle with magic. Don't even think about that Magician's Guild or whatever. Don't write to the duke for magic help. Don't ask his son to help us. Don't ask the Baron, or his son or anyone else. You don't need magic to have a child. You need to go back and wait until it's your turn. I'm not going to come to this magic woman's place and you shouldn't be going either." She stopped walking and crossed her arms over her chest.

Johanna glared at her and she glared back.

"So that's it? You don't care about our safety?"

"Have you listened to anything I said? About magic, about *my fault*?"

"I'm going to see this woman," she said, slowly, while looking into Loesie's eyes. "I understand that it could be dangerous. I understand that she is not 'just' a herb woman. But magic is happening whether we like it or not, and I can't see how not using it is going help us. In fact, I think it's going to be dangerous for us, because there is no place where we can hide where there is no magic. So you can show me that you care and help me deal with this magic, or you can go back to your sewing."

Loesie said nothing.

Johanna took a few steps in the direction of the town and looked over her shoulder. Loesie hadn't moved. Another few steps. She still hadn't moved.

Oh well, it was not to be helped.

Johanna continued towards the town without looking back.

The herb woman's house was on the other side of the markets, an old house that was so narrow that its façade had room only for a single door and one window. The walls had once been painted black, but much of the paint had flaked off, showing the stone underneath. This was a pretty common state of affairs for the houses in the town, and it was a very unremarkable house. So unremarkable, in fact, that it would be easy not to notice it at all. That was until you got close and saw the line of animal skulls and teeth on the windowsill. There were bird skulls with the beaks still attached, rabbit skulls, deer skulls with antlers, and skulls of larger animals. There was also, on a little shelf halfway across the window, a line of blackened triangular teeth. Some were smooth, some had serrated edges. Some of them were as long as her thumb. She wondered what kind of animal those teeth belonged to. Even the teeth on the bear skull were smaller.

The room on the other side of the window was too dark to see more than a few shapes inside. A couch and a formal sitting room chair, she thought.

The place felt a bit creepy, she had to admit. Maybe that was only because of all the warnings from Master Deim and Loesie. After all, anyone who studied the ways of nature would have skulls and bones from animals, and a herb woman studied nature, right?

Johanna put her hand on the wooden door. It showed her a woman going into the house carrying a child with a snotty nose. Another image showed an old man entering, leaning heavily on a walking stick.

See? Nothing to worry about. Just people going to see Magda with illnesses.

Johanna lifted the knocker in the shape of a deer skull and let the heavy metal thing fall on the wood. It made a heavy *thunk* that echoed in the hollow space beyond.

For a long time, nothing happened. Johanna was about to turn away. Perhaps the herb woman had gone out, but then there was a sound of shuffling footsteps behind the door.

A bolt was drawn back and the door opened, revealing a bent figure in the doorway, dressed in a grey cloak with a woollen scarf around her neck.

To Johanna's surprise, the face of the woman inside the shadow of the hood wasn't old at all. It was just badly stained with dark wine-red blotches, which were slightly raised, making the skin look like a giant lumpy strawberry. Johanna had seen people with these patches before, but never in such a prominent way. Her lumpy red skin surrounded one eye, covered her cheek down to the corner of her mouth, and it was also on the wrist and part of the hand that stuck out from underneath her cloak.

"Are you Magda?"

The woman replied in the local dialect, the tone not particularly friendly. Hilda had warned her about that.

"I'm sorry, I'm from Saarland. I don't speak your language. I was told to come here by Master Deim's sister-in-law Hilda."

"Ah. Hilda. Come," she said in a heavy accent.

Johanna went into the corridor, and Magda shut the door behind them, pushing the bolt back. It got very dark in the corridor, with just a faint glow of light coming in from a door that stood ajar at the end. Johanna presumed that this was the sitting room.

Magda grabbed her arm when she walked past and pulled her close. Her long nails dug into the soft skin on the underside of Johanna's upper arm. "Ow. There is no need to—"

"I know who you are. I can smell scent of betrayer on you."

Betrayer? "Sorry, I don't know what you're talking about." Her heart thudded like crazy. "I haven't spoken to anyone in town." Did she mean Duke Lothar, or the Baroness or Sylvan or Kylian?

"You ignorant girl. Don't think I don't know that you spy on me."

"Please, I'm not here for anyone except myself," Johanna said. "I . . ." She was going to say *need your help*, but after that exchange wasn't sure that what she'd be getting would qualify as "help" and even less whether she'd need it. "Hilda said that you were good with herbs."

Magda let go of her arm with a snort, muttering something in her dialect. The look in her eyes was pure venom.

"Hmph." She stepped back and regarded Johanna with her red-blotched face. "Herbs, huh?"

"Yes. For making tea. Raspberry leaves, and stinging nettles."

"Herbs," she repeated, her face still suspicious. "Well then, let's talk about herbs."

Johanna followed her down a dark corridor where their footsteps were muffled by a series of bearskins on the floor, the fur all matted and dirty. Dusty tapestries on the walls depicted a family tree, a hunting scene and a castle in the forest which could have been Duke Lothar's, but it was too dark to see. They came out in a dark room with a single window at the back of the house. It looked out over the house in the next street, across a narrow alley.

The light was so dim in the room that even in daylight it was hard to see. The ceiling and the floorboards and threadbare carpet were all dark. Around the walls were shelves to the ceiling filled with jars and pots. Each contained some powder, leaves or various dried items or items preserved in fluid. The air in the room smelled stale and dirty, with a tang of dried leaves and a waft of something dead.

The shelves left just enough room for a round table and a couple of chairs, all very well-worn and dusty.

At Magda's invitation, she squeezed between the shelves and the chairs.

Magda sat opposite Johanna with her back to the window. She slowly lowered the hood of her cloak. Her red-rimmed eye was blue, but her other eye was all white, like Loesie's had been when she was struck by magic. The wine red stain extended across her face, her neck and chest. Likely it covered all of her shoulder and left arm as well.

Johanna didn't know where to look. Staring would be impolite, but purposely looking away would be impolite, too.

When sitting down, Johanna made the mistake of touching the table. A stream of images went through her. The people who had sat at this table were mostly men, and they weren't sick. They came to talk. They were monks and priests and men in plain clothes. Men in dark clothes with long beards. Johanna withdrew her hand from the table, her heart thudding.

Magda was smiling at her. "Ah. I see. There is a pitiful amount of magic in you. Well, let's talk, then. About *herbs*."

Johanna took a calming breath. "I've been with my husband for over three months. I am still not with child."

"Three months, huh?"

"I've lain with my husband every day. I thought for a while that it worked, but my bleeding started yesterday. It's very important that I have a child as soon as possible. There are . . . people who don't accept our marriage unless there is a child and they want to do everything they can to prevent that from happening."

It seemed so long ago that she'd been adamant that she didn't want to get married, but now she could see why Father had said that society wouldn't accept her. Once the marriage was declared invalid, she would never marry again, and without a business to run—was there even anything left in Saardam?—she would have no income. "It's really important. You have to understand."

"Oh, I understand important. Important means you want something and you believe someone can give it to you."

"Well, I . . ."

Magda pointed a red-skinned finger at her. "Important means that you believe you should get something. But forget that some things are not ours to give."

"I know that. I just thought you would have some herbs that might help."

"Hmm. I could give you some herbs for tea, yes." Magda rose and started rummaging on the shelves. She took off a large jar and then another one. Then she unfolded a triangular paper bag from a drawer and put a scoop full of dried leaves in each.

While this was happening, Johanna looked around the room. There was a stone tile leaning against the wall with writing on it in a language Johanna didn't recognise. There was also a carving depicting a head of some sort of creature.

"Here are herbs," Magda said, pushing the folded bag across the table to Johanna. "Make tea. Drink every morning and every evening."

"Thank you."

And because there seemed nothing else to say, Johanna gathered up the paper bag and made to get up. To be honest, she felt keen to get out of here.

"That's all?"

"What do you mean?"

Magda's form was backlit by the window. "Is that all you come to talk about? Herbs?"

"Well, I . . ." She had intended to ask about the Magician's Guild and getting a court magician, but in between Loesie's strange behaviour and Master Deim's warning, she was not so sure anymore. If there was one true thing about Loesie's words, it was that Johanna really knew nothing about magic and she didn't know what she was playing with.

"Well . . . what if it doesn't work, the tea?"

Magda gave Johanna a sharp look. "First you ask for herbs. Then you say herbs don't work?"

"I'm sorry, I—"

"Herb medicine have two parts: one is the herb, two is the belief that it will work. No belief, no work."

Johanna frowned.

"If you want to know if you're doing it right with your man, then I can't help. I know nothing about being with a man. Do you see a man here? Do you think I can get man ugly like this?" She angled her face to the light so that the red lumpy skin was more visible.

"I never said—"

"No, but you *think* and I can see what you think because I seen it all my life. I seen people not know where to look."

Johanna decided to plunge in anyway. She hadn't come here only to chicken out again. Saardam was facing hard issues, and there weren't going to be easy solutions. "I was wondering if my inability to get with child could have a magical cause because I'm pretty sure we're doing everything right."

"Ha! Magic! You know nothing about magic." An odd, happy, vindicated tone crept into her voice.

"That's why I'm here: to ask you."

"Magic comes with life and nature. Magic is all around. You people talk about *believing* in magic, but it is not something you can *believe* in. Magic is still going to be there, even if you don't *believe*. Because magic is real." Magda waved a finger in front of Johanna's face. "You people, people from Church, they just scared. Church says they can't use magic and magic people are bad. Bah. But yes, magic is cause of not being with child, because magic is cause of *everything*. Magic is why we alive."

"Then . . . could you use magic to solve it? I understand it will cost more."

Magda laughed, not a pleasant sound. "You understand nothing, little queen. You do not understand at all." She got up from her seat. She squeezed past Loesie and went to a cupboard along the wall. When she opened the door, Johanna could see rows of jars of substances: bright yellow powder, rust red powder, white things that looked like little twigs, curly things that looked like lizard tails, a jar full of blue and grey spotted eggs, another full of frog skulls and many other strange things.

She took out a stone basin on a stand, an earthenware pot with a lid and a blue glass bottle with a clear liquid sloshing inside.

She placed the basin in the middle of the table, unstoppered the bottle and poured in a small measure of fluid. It looked like water, but spread a sharp scent through the room that made Johanna feel dizzy, like strong spirits. Then she took the lid off the pot and sprinkled some of its contents, a fine white powder, in the water. Whatever the fine powder was, it made the fluid bubble and smoke.

Magda leaned over the basin and breathed the vapour. She had closed her eyes. The lumpy red skin even covered her eyelid.

For a while, nothing happened. Johanna glanced over her shoulder at the door. It was still open, in case she wanted to get out quickly.

Then Magda opened her eyes. Both of them had gone white.

Magda started speaking. "Give me your hand, so I can read your magic lines." Her voice sounded rough and intense, and made a chill run down Johanna's back.

Johanna hesitated. If there was some dark magic to keep her from becoming with child, she wanted to know about it. That was why she had come here.

She held out her hand.

Magda gasped. The white mist fled her eyes. "Who is your master?"

"I have no master. I've met Duke Lothar and I watched while he exorcised a demon from my friend. Maybe you can feel that—"

"You disturb the magic lines. Who is your master?" Her voice was more intense now.

"I have no idea what you mean. I'm sorry."

"You ignorant people. Then what is your bloodline?"

"My mother came from the Aroden court." She didn't think there were any strong magicians in that family. Just some people who, like her, could read things in wind or wood. She wasn't even sure that her mother could do this.

Magda said nothing for a while, breathing the fumes from the basin until her eyes went white again. "I feel, I feel . . . could be the betrayer's presence. Could be, could be. Don't know why it would be so strong in you. Maybe you care for the betrayer, huh?"

"I'm afraid I have no idea who you're talking about."

"The one with the two faces." The white eyes met Johanna's, causing a chill to run over her back.

"Who is this person? Do I need to be careful of him? Is it someone in the camp?"

"Ha. You do not know anything."

"I don't. Tell me who this person is."

"The mention of the name would kill me. Magic so strong that none of us can fight it. That's what happens when you disturb magic lines. When you dig up magic from soil where it should never be disturbed."

That was exactly what Loesie had been talking about. "How have people disturbed the magic lines?"

"They dug it out of the soil."

"Where?"

"You do not want to know. It is an evil place for innocent girls. It is no good talking about it because we cannot do anything about it. Even we are powerless."

We? Wait— "Are you from the Magician's Guild?" That would make an awful lot of sense, including the visitors in dark clothes she had seen sitting at this table.

Magda hissed, which Johanna took as an admission. She said nothing in reply, but didn't deny connections with the Magician's Guild either.

"Please, we need your help. The king needs a court magician."

Magda laughed, not a pretty sound. "The king needs a court magician as much as he needs a jester. A court magician *is* a jester. We do not perform *tricks*." She held up an ugly, red-skinned finger.

"Then whatever you want to call it. We need help."

"Every person in this world needs help."

"I would like you to help us."

Magda was silent for a long time and after a while Johanna feared that she wasn't going to respond at all. She was constantly moving her hands over the bowl.

Johanna stared at those hands, wondering what Magda was doing, wondering if it would be impolite or dangerous to interrupt her and ask her more forcefully. She just wanted an answer. Yes or no, a reply she could act on.

But now something was happening in the bowl. The trails of vapour thickened around Magda's fingers and dripped off back into the basin, forming shapes. Misty forms coalesced into buildings and boats, and people. Her hands were weaving a town out of mist. Was that Saardam? If so, what was that strange ship in the harbour? It was much bigger than any of the local ships, even the seafaring ones, and two really thick masts.

The white vapour had added a building to the town with a dome that towered over the surrounding houses. That had to be either the re-built palace or a new church. The Church of the Triune didn't go for splendour, so it was either the palace or . . . a place of worship for the Belaman Church. She shivered. "Is that mist showing me the future?"

"What mist?" Magda withdrew her hands.

The vapour dissipated and the city of mist fell back into the basin. Johanna stared at the mirror-like surface of the fluid. Not a ripple.

"You did not see any mist," Magda said.

"Um, I'm not sure."

"When people ask, you saw no mist. You saw no buildings and you saw no ships."

"All right, yes."

"I showed this because you will understand danger. Now go and don't play with magic ever again."

"Sure." Johanna rose, taking the paper bag with dried leaves off the table. "Thank you for the leaves. I'm . . . I'll make the tea as soon as I get back." She couldn't think. It was as if that mist had gone straight into her head. Magda rested her hands on the table, the fingers interlaced, but Johanna swore she could still see the fingers weaving the mist over the basin.

She saw the large ship in the harbour, and such a panic took hold of her that she couldn't breathe.

This was the future or something that was happening right now. With all her mind, she wanted to be back home, to look for Father, to help Roald take up his rightful position, to save the town from whatever evil had come in that ship. Loesie said that the magic lines had been disturbed. That ship was the disturbance. She and the others were wasting her time here. They were needed at home.

Johanna stumbled from the room. Magda said something, but the sound of her voice became lost in the roaring of blood in her ears. She walked through the dark corridor, tripping over one of the bearskin mats and into the street.

When she was at the porch, she realised what Magda had said: "You will have two children."

CHAPTER 11

I T WAS NOT until Johanna was in the market square that the fog lifted from her mind and she could think clearly and tease out the things that Magda had told her. Most of it was more or less what Loesie had said: something disturbed magic lines and no one is powerful enough to fix it. But someone had done this while digging. And there was a strange ship in the harbour in Saardam, possibly belonging to Alexandre.

That was more information than she'd had before, but it was still very incomplete.

The sky was darker than it had been when she came in, but right now, only a steady drizzle fell from the solid layer of clouds, whipped up by squalls of wind that chased the low-hanging clouds over the jumble of slate-covered roofs.

The heavy clouds promised more rain, and she had better hurry up if she wanted to stay dry.

She was about halfway along the riverbank when the clouds started disgorging their contents. Big fat drops fell. Johanna ran close to whatever little shelter the meagre bushes along the path offered, but quite a few drops still fell on her scarf. Wet spots were starting to seep through.

Then the rain struck in all earnest. The wind whipped up. So much water fell down from the sky that it was hard to see. Within a few paces she was soaked through.

On this part of the path from the outskirts of town to the camp there was no shelter at all. Sheets of rain lashed the trees.

Shards of mist rose from the river and drifted over the field. They *moved*.

Johanna stopped. She stood staring at the river, with the rain pelting down and water dripping from her hair. The water churned like it was boiling.

Johanna retreated.

Out of the mist rose an animal: a white-winged swan that glided over the water.

Then another one.

Both birds looked real and yet they did not. Their feathers were too bright, their beaks too orange.

Swans built their nests in the reed beds on the riverbank and she would have noticed their nest when coming this way. Swans were usually very defensive of those nests. There would have been cygnets, by now adult-sized but still with their grey feathers, aggressively defended by both parents. She knew a boy who got bitten by a swan so badly that his pants needed mending.

As she watched, both birds took to the air with a grace she had never seen from birds this large. She had only ever seen swans run over the water before they flew. It usually happened with much splashing and flapping of wings.

There were no ripples on the water. Already, both birds had vanished from sight.

But now something else appeared out of the mist: a figure of a woman, dressed in a light-coloured cloak with a hood covering her head. She was floating towards the shore, appearing to walk over the water.

Before she reached the riverbank, the ghostly figure veered to the left and floated in the direction of the camp.

Johanna felt cold.

If this was the ghost of Celine again, she could only imagine the mayhem and panic that would cause in the camp.

She quickened her pace and ran through the mud. The ghost had disappeared between the reeds, which had combed deposits of grass and twigs out of the water.

Was Johanna imagining things or had the river level risen a lot since she'd come here on the way into town?

A scream echoed over the water, a woman or a child.

Johanna ran, but that wasn't easy in the sodden clothes. Her muscles were stiff with the cold and the rain had made the path muddy and slippery.

In amongst the reeds stood some boys. Against the advice of the adults, they had gone to play by the river, and one of them was pointing in the direction of the water.

Another boy picked up a stone and threw it at the ghost. The projectile fell far short. He picked up another stone.

"No, don't!" His friend held his arm back.

"Why? It's a ghost."

"Don't you see? It's Princess Celine!"

The boy let his arm sink, staring open-mouthed at the ghost.

One of the younger boys started to cry.

The woman turned and she met Johanna's eyes squarely. It was indeed the same apparition she had seen in the library. Johanna wanted to run, but a strange fascination kept her standing on the riverbank. She wanted to run and . . . what? No one would help her. No one even believed that this ghost existed, that it recognised her.

There was a voice behind her. "Don't get close to that one. That's not a normal ghost."

Loesie stood higher up the riverbank, her arms crossed over her chest and her hair whipped up by the wind.

"That's the witch!" a boy yelled, pointing at Loesie.

"Shoo with you," Loesie called. "Run to your mothers. This is no sight for little boys."

"Leave Celine alone. She's our princess."

Johanna said in a kinder voice, "This isn't Celine, it's an apparition. A ghost. It could be dangerous. Please do as the lady says."

One of the oldest boys said, "What do you know? That's a witch, not a lady, and you're not even the real queen anyway. My father says so." He was at that age where boys are tall and gangly, all angles and awkwardness, with a mop of unruly blond hair. He looked like a ragamuffin, but the shirt he had gotten covered in mud was well-made. This was no ship's boy.

A younger, soft-faced boy said, "Is that why she's all white? Because she's a ghost?"

Johanna said, "Yes, and also why she won't answer your questions."

The older boy said again, "She can't be a ghost, because she already answered our questions. She says she's the real princess and you and the Idiot King can't take her place."

Another boy added, in a quiet voice, "My mother says ghosts don't exist anyway and they're all figments of the imagination of witches to scare us."

Johanna wondered where he had learned such big words.

They descended into an argument, their shrill voices echoing over the water.

The blond boy gestured at the apparition, which had retreated a bit from the riverbank. "If she's not a ghost, what do you think that is, then? Isn't she walking on the water?"

"Yes," the shy boy said.

"Can you walk over water?"

"No, but she's a princess. Maybe she can."

"The king can't walk on water."

"How do you know?"

"Oh, come on, stop being silly. People can't walk on water. Ghosts can float wherever they please."

"Oh, look!" A little boy pointed over the water.

The ghostly woman was now coming towards the river-bank, her eyes burning with anger.

Johanna pushed the younger boys up the river bank. "Please listen to us and go to your mothers. It's not safe here."

The boys moved a bit up the riverbank, but stopped there to watch.

The ghost kept coming for Johanna. The closer she came, the more the flesh of her face sagged. The folds and canyons in the skin deepened, the skin pitted and scarred. She no longer looked like Celine, but like a skull with two gaping holes from which green light radiated.

Behind her, the boys screamed and ran, but Johanna stood rooted to the ground. Her knees felt like they would collapse on her if she took a single step.

"There you are again," the raspy voice said. "You usurper. You common girl. Let you be cursed!" She pointed at Johanna with a discoloured, bony hand, uttering guttural sounds that resembled no spoken words. Green light flashed along the fingers, dripping off as if the skin itself turned liquid. Strands of silver-green coalesced into a giant spider web.

Johanna ducked. She landed on her knees in the tall grass with a loud *splosh*. Cold water seeped through her dress.

Loesie retreated against the trunk of a sapling. She broke off a twig at her back and waved it before her.

"I will get you, little queen." The ghost laughed, a wheezy sound that made a chill crawl over Johanna's back. The form of her was still changing. She discarded the grey cloak and the pale yellow dress. The skin underneath was lumpy and scarred. Her legs had turned into sticks. Buds sprouted from her waist, growing into long and thin legs with hair along the sides. The head grew two big fangs. The body inflated until it was fat and round, like that of a spider, but many times bigger.

A spider that was throwing out its sticky threads to reel in its victims.

Loesie lashed out at the web. The willow twigs went straight through the threads without leaving a mark but the twig ignited in Loesie's hand. Threads of spider silk wrapped around Loesie's chest, pinning her arms to her sides.

"Loesie, no!"

Johanna stumbled to her feet, but no matter how much she tried to grab the strands that held Loesie, her hands kept going through the material as if the threads weren't there.

Loesie's eyes had gone white again, rolled back into her head. Her back was rigid like a plank of wood.

Johanna called out, "Help! Help me!"

But the boys had run, and the camp was too far away for anyone to hear.

Then without warning, the spider-ghost vanished. The web retreated. Loesie dropped into the grass causing Johanna to fall on top of her.

Oof.

Johanna lay there for a while, dazed, while the trails of mist were reabsorbed back into the water.

"Loesie?"

Loesie's eyes had returned to normal. She wiped her face.

"Loesie, are you all right? Do you know why it disappeared suddenly?"

"That was no common magic." Loesie's voice sounded hoarse. "That was no proper ghost."

"Did it leave because of something you did?"

Loesie laughed. "Like I wave a willow twig and all the evil in the world flees from my sight? Wouldn't that be handy?" She coughed.

They sat silently in the grass while a steady drizzle came down. Water was seeping into the back of Johanna's dress.

"Loesie, can you see now that I need a magician to help men, and I'm asking you to be that magician?"

Loesie's expression closed. "Can't you see that magic is no good, and you don't want to meddle with it?"

"Please. I don't have anyone else I can trust. Even if you just take the position until we can find someone else."

"I'm no magician. I'm struck mad by magic. And you shouldn't be trusting me. That's the last I'll say about it."

Johanna didn't understand it. For years, Loesie had come to the markets flaunting her magic. Loesie's magic ran much deeper than the little tricks she used to scare off little boys. She had never been one to hide it, talking about the warnings against magic by the church as *They don't know what they're talking about* and *Magic is not something you can stop. It's there or it isn't, no matter what the gibbering priests say.*

Johanna used to talk with her about that, because the preachings of Shepherd Romulus about magic didn't sit well with her, either. Now it seemed like Loesie had completely closed to magic. What had changed her mind?

Surely it wouldn't really be about magic lines and increasing magic, because she didn't believe that for one bit.

She helped Loesie up and the two of them continued along the riverbank, Loesie moving like an old woman.

CHAPTER 12

THE STORY that the boys had seen princess Celine went around the camp like wildfire.

By the end of that afternoon, a group of people, mainly women, had gathered at the spot in the reeds where the boys had seen Celine, and they stood on the bank, staring over the water. A steady drizzle of rain fell from the sky, but that didn't seem to bother them.

At first, Johanna had tried to explain that what the boys had seen was an evil construct of magic, but although the women listened politely, none of them said anything or asked any questions, and none of them went back to the camp.

Johanna looked around that circle of tired-looking, pale faces and empty eyes, wet and bedraggled clothes that had seen better days. A shiver came over her. No one had seen the green light coming from the skull-like eyes. No one had seen the spider. No one had seen how it had grabbed hold of Loesie and turned her rigid. And Johanna didn't know how to alert people to the danger. Most people tolerated Loesie while she behaved normally, but Johanna had heard some rumours about her that indicated that people knew very well who she was.

Waiting and doing nothing had turned these people numb. Or so she hoped, because the empty look in their eyes reminded her uncomfortably of Loesie's expression when she had first met Loesie in the market, when Loesie had been possessed.

What did it even look like when a demon entered a person's body?

Or was it something in the air? Magic lines coming to the surface? Where did this magic even come from?

Johanna went back and watched the group from the deck of the *Lady Sara*, with frustration growing inside her.

"What has gotten into these people?" she said to Nellie who had come out of the cabin. "They never wanted to have anything to do with magic before." They were mainly women and children, but also some younger men, staring at the water with dreamy expressions in their eyes. Occasionally one would point and the others would squint into the mist. A woman folded her hands as if in prayer.

Nellie said, "I've never seen these people inside the Church of the Triune."

"No, there is only one church they follow: that of money."

"You shouldn't say things like that, mistress Johanna. These people have lost everything. Their safe houses, their servants, their nice furniture, their beautiful clothes. They don't know how to look after themselves. They're looking for guidance."

"And they're getting that from a ghost that's a spider in disguise?" Johanna spread her hands. "Sometimes I really can't believe how dumb people are, even those who are supposed to know better."

"The people are desperate. They do desperate things."

"Nellie, I love you and you're a much better woman than I

am, but sometimes I wish you could just believe that sometimes people do things for stupid reasons. Or evil reasons, or selfish reasons."

"I'd rather be accused of being too good than being too selfish and inconsiderate. Anyway, I came to look for you because we need to take some measurements for your wedding dress."

Johanna followed Nellie into the cabin.

It turned out that Nellie had been able to get some nice fabric from a seller at the markets. She got it for a good price because, according to the seller, no one was sure what to do with the fabric. It was quite stiff but of rough weave, like linen. Nellie showed it to her just outside the door to the captain's cabin, because *it's too dark in there to see it properly*. Johanna ran her hand over the fabric. It was rough and well-made at the same time, if that was possible, and it made her think of the exotic markets she had visited on her trip to Lurezia with Father. Those fabrics spoke of strange lands where the sun rode high in the sky and where the land was covered in sand dunes as far as the eye could see. It was rather odd that something as exotic as this had been cheap, and they might discover that there was something wrong with it, but what could be wrong with a piece of fabric?

There was one problem: it was red.

"Then we shall have to make red lace," Nellie said.

Judging by the pins and cushion on the table, she had already started the tedious work of making lace.

"Oh no, that's Loesie's," she said when she noticed Johanna looking at the work.

"It's nice."

"Yes, she is getting much better, and making a lot of effort to learn, too."

That was Loesie these days: doing everything to prove that she was just a normal, non-magical farm girl so that she could go on resisting Johanna's pleas to learn about magic and be Roald's court magician.

Loesie herself was on the deck hanging out the washing. As if she felt Johanna looking at her, she turned her head so that their eyes met through the little round window.

Nellie had managed to collect a gathering of sewing things, for which Loesie had made a basket. She bustled about with measuring tape, taking measurements across Johanna's back both lengthwise and sideways. She measured around Johanna's waist. "We shall leave a spare fold of fabric here that we can take out in case you need it."

Yes, yes, she got the hint.

"Nellie, do you know what is going on with Loesie?"

"Going on? Nothing. Since we left that horrible house of the Duke's she has been extremely helpful and kind. I can see her turn into a very useful servant."

But that was just the problem. Johanna didn't *need* another useful servant, and *useful servant* had not ever been words anyone would use to describe Loesie.

"Well, I guess you never knew Loesie before the . . . accident."

"I guess not, but I'd say that she's finally seen sense and quit that childish teasing and making fun of boys." Nellie's voice was prim. "Is it wrong to teach her sewing?"

"No, not at all."

"I just thought I'd teach her to be useful."

"You're doing fine, Nellie. I'm sure the dress will be beautiful."

After some talk about arrangements for clothing for Roald, because *What he wears is completely unsuitable for a king. No wonder people don't take him seriously*, Johanna left Nellie to continue with her work.

To be honest, she didn't really want to have an official wedding; she wanted to return to Saardam. She wanted to know what was going on there. And she was getting quite worried about those young men who had taken Master Deim's dinghy and had still not returned, and she had become even more worried with Loesie's explanation, which had been confirmed by Magda: magic was leaking out of the ground. Loesie said that the Saar River had always been rich in magic and she wondered if, since water came out of the ground, magic could come up with the water. Magda said someone had been digging.

Why would anyone dig for magic? Or if they weren't digging for magic, what would they dig for? What would they do about the magic now that they'd found it?

A strange thought came to her: *use it*. Use the magic to defeat all their enemies.

If you couldn't fight magic without invoking more magic, then wasn't the next logical step to use that magic?

Johanna slid open the hold cover and descended into the darkness and its perpetual smell of dust.

Roald sat writing over the tiny desk, his silhouette gilded by the light. It didn't look like he had moved since she left him here in the morning.

Johanna took off her wet cloak and hung it on the hook under the stairs.

Roald didn't even glance aside, so she went up and looked over his shoulder at the book he was reading.

On Magickal Creatures Of The High Lands, The Sea And Orient, one of the books she had borrowed from Brother Reginald.

The page showed a couple of illustrations of huge lizards with wings and strange, snake-like beings that devoured ships. "What strange creatures."

"They're sea dragons and land dragons," Roald said. "It says here that dragon magic is the highest form of magic and rules all others."

Johanna studied the scaled creatures, with huge spiky heads and lots of sharp teeth. "I've never seen creatures like this."

She would have said that they didn't exist, but after seeing the magical spider, she wasn't sure anymore. There were lands unknown beyond the Horn that harboured the strangest of creatures. She also didn't know if "exist" was the right word for a being that was a figment of magic. If magicians could create what they wanted, then the ghost-ether could be shaped into any form.

"They had a small dragon at the farm," Roald said.

"Did you see it?"

"I had to feed it. It was about this big." He held his hands about an arm's length apart.

"Did it fly?"

"No, but it bites."

"Where did it come from?"

"The lands beyond the Horn. The abbot bought it from some peddler who came to sell silk and linen."

"Why was it there? Was it a magical being?"

"Brother Lucius keeps it as a pet. It sits on his shoulder. It warns him if the air is starting to go bad."

"Go bad?"

"Sometimes the air explodes. The dragon makes noises when it smells the bad air so the people can get out."

"What sort of place is this?" She had never heard of exploding air.

"At the farm."

"Yes, but what sort of place at the farm?"

"At the chapel in the valley behind the fields. Mist comes out of the ground. They're building an oracle room to surround it."

"Mist or ghosts?"

"Never saw a ghost in all the time I was there."

Johanna pulled out the map of the town and surrounding forest that Roald had bought from a mapmaker at the markets. She rolled it out on the desk. The map was a thing of beauty, precisely made with the finest pen strokes.

The town of Florisheim was on the eastern bank of the Rede River, while the lower areas on the western side, part of Burovia, were mostly wild land of marshes and forests. To her, this very much started to sound like the people there had been digging up the magic lines and Roald had either not seen it or dismissed it as something he didn't want to deal with.

On the map, the farm was marked with only a little black square. Underneath, it said in tiny letters: *Order of the Guentherites*.

Johanna pointed at the spot. "Is that what they're called? The Guentherites?"

"Brother Guenther was the abbot. He was very old and died while I was there. I didn't see him much because he was always sick. He's the second cousin of Baron Uti. He inherited the land to the south of here, and had to battle Duke Lothar for the rights to the castle. He lost, so he started the farm."

"Did he build it? Did no one live there before?"

"No. Because the land was haunted."

She would ask him whether this order was officially recognised by the Belaman Church, but he probably wouldn't understand the intricacies involved in church relationships. So she let the topic rest, but she was becoming more and more certain that a lot of the trouble in the world came back to this farm and its magic lines.

"Would you want to go and visit the farm?"

Roald turned to her, frowning. "Why?"

"Well, because . . . because you know people there. Because you have friends there?"

He stared at her, as if his brain was processing the concept of *friends*. "Does that mean I would see Selmus?"

"That depends on if he's still there." She had no idea who this person was, but found some relief in knowing that Roald had made at least one friend. "Do people from the farm visit Florisheim?"

"They do, if the abbot lets you go. You need two strong rowers."

And rowing across the river was not going to happen while the water was so high. But they had sea cows and could use them. "Do people visit?"

"Only important people."

"That's easy, then. As soon as the water calms a bit, we will announce a visit so that you can see Selmus."

But the rains kept up, and although the water levels dropped a bit, the river remained a churning mass of water. Visiting that farm seemed like it might create more problems than she could deal with. Over the next week increasing numbers of people came to the riverbank where the boys had seen Celine. Someone put up a wooden post in the water with a platform on top and the next day a little statue appeared there, whittled from wood, and depicting a woman. It was a rough and coarsely-made thing, but the long hair and cloak made it clear that this represented Princess Celine. People stood at the riverbank and gazed at it. Some people even brought small offerings: flowers or whatever scraps of food they could spare. The riverbank became muddy and trampled, and the ever-rising waters came closer and closer to the platform.

"I didn't think that the nobles were this superstitious,"

Johanna said to Master Deim while watching this strange going-on from the deck.

It had stopped raining and the river was still high, only a few hand-widths under the deck of the jetty, but when the sun broke through the clouds, it didn't look as threatening.

"It's a feature of the Belaman Church to worship ghosts. They call them saints, but it's all the same thing."

That same Belaman Church that had a saint for mothers and babies, the church that was ever-present in all of life in Florisheim, and an institute that Johanna didn't understand. There had been a small Belaman Church building in Saardam, but it was modest, nothing like the magnificent construction in the market place.

"Are you ready to go to the council meeting?" Master Deim said.

"I'm ready. I got Roald ready earlier this morning. I'll go and get him." She went down into the hold where Roald sat with his head buried in a book as usual.

Until Nellie and Loesie had made him new clothes, his best garment was the red velvet jacket that he had worn on the night of their escape from Saardam. These days, it was more brown than red. The dunking in the harbour hadn't done it much good, and the dirt had become so engrained in the fabric that even Nellie's scrubbing wouldn't budge it. On a day like this, it was also quite hot, but one of the oddities about Roald was that he never, ever, removed or put on an item of clothing by himself.

"Come, Roald, we need to go."

He ignored her.

She went down the stairs and put an arm on his shoulders. "Come. The council is waiting for us."

"The meeting is stupid."

She agreed with him, but if she said so, he was likely to blurt it all over the camp. "We have to go."

"I don't want to."

"Please, Roald. You're the king." She gently pulled his arm.

"No." His muscles stiffened. "Those men don't like me and I don't like them. They talk about me behind my back and laugh at me. They call me The Idiot King. I am the king, and I am not going to talk to people who are rude to me."

There was nothing Johanna could say to that. She wasn't going to assure him that no, this was not the case at all. The men *did* talk behind his back and they *did* call him The Idiot King. How to change that would be the big challenge, but it probably wouldn't be fought in the Council of Nobles. The rot had probably started with King Nicholaos and his son wasn't going to change anything.

"Is there a problem?" Master Deim asked at the top of the stairs.

"He doesn't want to come."

"The meeting is stupid! I want to go catching frogs." He had that determined look in his eyes.

Johanna glanced at Master Deim. What to do?

"Leave him," Master Deim said. "He wouldn't do our cause justice. Not like this. We'll go by ourselves and say that he's unwell."

Johanna could agree with that, but what would the nobles say? Worse, how bad would the gossip get?

Johanna followed Master Deim off the gangplank. The sentries posted there greeted both of them. Every time Johanna passed these men—and there were four taking turns —she felt less easy about why they were here. They were Johan Delacoeur's men and the aims of the nobles and of Johanna and Roald started to diverge increasingly.

It might be time to speak to Julianna again about finding guards in the camp who were more loyal to the throne.

By the time Johanna and Master Deim arrived at the boat

shed, Master Deim's high forehead glistened with sweat. Big clouds built again on the horizon, so it was likely that there would be more rain.

All the council members were already seated around the table. They had been talking, but fell silent when Johanna and Master Deim came in.

Fleuris LaFontaine raised his eyebrows.

"The king is indisposed," Master Deim said. "There has been an illness of the stomach going around the camp."

There were some nods around the table. Johan Delacoeur seemed happy. He eyed Ignatius Hemeldinck, and a smile ghosted over Ignatius' face.

Johanna sat down at the position that would normally be Roald's. "The king has authorised me to take care of his affairs." She looked around the table, and it struck her that someone else was missing. "Where is the Shepherd Carolus?"

"Late, probably," Fleuris LaFontaine said. Yes, it was true that he'd been late at the first meeting, too.

"Should we send someone out to get him?" Johanna asked.

"I'll ask Pieter," Master Deim said.

He rose from the table. Pieter was one of Johan Delacoeur's men, and this meant that Master Deim had to walk back to the *Lady Sara* and would be gone for a while.

Johanna made sure that the first subject of discussion was something relatively harmless: the upcoming wedding.

The Baroness Viktoriya had sent her servants to inform Johanna of the arrangements, and frankly she felt that the entire ceremony was out of her control. She had even supplied a priest, because *You have to be married in a civilised church*, and somehow Johanna expected a summons to appear that the day prior to the wedding, she'd be expected to come to the Belaman Church to convert.

"I'd like to hold something more intimate for our own

people as well. I'd like the Shepherd Carolus to conduct a ceremony."

Distaste flickered over Ignatius' face. "We will lose support from the Baron if we persist with that church."

"It is *our* church," Johanna said.

It was the church of Saardam, the church of the common people. Not the nobles. Not the Baron's church. Not the church of pomp and ceremony and the church that was richer than many royal families.

"I would like a brief ceremony just for our people, held on the deck of the *Prosperity* or if there is not enough room, in the camp. We can hold it on the day of the other feast, or the day before."

"I'm not in favour of holding it on the riverfront," Johan Delacoeur said. "These days, gatherings of people along the waterfront seem to attract an increasing number of ghost sightings."

Johanna's heart jumped. "Have there been any more apparitions?"

"If my wife is to be believed, yes. She says if you go out at dusk and look into the reeds at a certain angle, you will see where the ghost sleeps."

Ignatius laughed. "And you believe this, too?"

"Apparently, a lot of women have seen this apparition of Celine," Johan Delacoeur said. His voice let little doubt about what he thought of this development.

"It is rumoured that King Nicholaos was trying to have her resurrected," Fleuris LaFontaine said.

Ignatius laughed again. "Nonsense."

Johan held up his finger like a teacher. "Whether it's true or not doesn't matter. It's what the people believe and we'll have to deal with it."

"Can't we just . . . remove the whole damn shrine thing

overnight?" Ignatius Hemeldinck said. "Kick it over so that it falls in the water?"

"No, we can't." Johanna was surprised by the amount of anger in her voice. If she had learned anything from Nellie, it was not to disrespect what other people felt, or at least not in public.

He harrumphed. "It's a thing to keep the women busy. Nothing substantial."

And you wonder why you're not married?

Fleuris LaFontaine said, "You can't take it away and not have a lot of trouble and protest. I don't like it either. My wife is taken with the thing, even though she never saw the apparition of Celine. If you take it away, all the womenfolk will be angry with us." He might be a boor, but he wasn't stupid.

Ignatius snorted.

"You will *not* take it away." Johanna met his eyes, a hard expression in them. Oh, he hated to be ordered by a woman. He didn't think Roald should be issuing orders, but he thought even less of her.

Master Deim returned a bit later, without Shepherd Carolus. "I can't find him anywhere. He's probably gone harvesting somewhere."

This was met with comments of *probably*, and the meeting continued.

Besides the wedding, and the "proper" ceremony, the council discussed arrangements for the running of the camp. With the wet weather, straw was becoming short in supply, and so much of the field was muddy that some tents had been moved to the other side of the road. This land belonged to a grumpy farmer who wanted a heavy payment for the use of his paddock. The council discussed options: move to yet another field or move to more permanent housing in town.

The latter option confirmed Johanna's suspicion that many of the nobles had little interest in returning to Saardam.

By the time the meeting ended, Shepherd Carolus had still not turned up.

"Does he often completely forget the meeting?" Johanna asked Master Deim while they were walking back along the riverbank.

"He usually remembers at some time. He's not been this late before." Master Deim gazed over the curve of the river, as if expecting to see the Shepherd come running towards the boat shed with hay in his hair but the path ahead was and remained empty.

"I saw him this morning," Captain Arense said.

"Did he mention the meeting?"

"No, but he did say that he was going to meet someone from town to speak about shoes for children."

"That sounds like him," Master Deim said. "He's probably just forgotten."

They passed the shrine to Celine. Three women stood watching it, one of them holding the hands of two children too young to play. None of the women prayed or cried. They just watched. Bathed in sunlight, the scene didn't look so disturbing. Johanna was reminded of the statues of the saints in the church with the flowers and the candles and velvet-covered seats. Most of the nobles had grown up with the Belaman Church and might view it in the same way. To them, Celine had turned into a saint.

If Johanna hadn't seen the apparition turn into a spider-like monster, she would have thought nothing of it.

The women greeted Johanna and Master Deim with polite nods of the head, and one of the children said, "Oh, look. It's the queen."

The mothers greeted her with polite nods and Johanna

returned their greeting. When she and Master Deim had passed, the women went back to staring at the shrine.

"I still don't know what to think about that thing," she said to Master Deim when they were walking around the reed bed.

"It gives them hope," Master Deim said. "Something to pray to that their families are still alive."

"I'm afraid that one day, that monstrous thing will return and kill all of them." She looked into Master Deim's eyes. "This land is soaking in magic. We're not equipped to deal with it. We need to go back to our own land as soon as possible. Before winter comes."

He nodded.

"You will come with us, won't you?" The thought of leaving him here made her chest constrict with panic. With Father not here, he had become like a second a father to her. "I wish we got some news about what is going on in Saardam. Why do you think those scouts we sent haven't come back yet?"

Master Deim gazed over the churning water of the river. "There could be any number of reasons, but I have to admit I don't like it much."

"No." Johanna shook her head.

They looked over the river for a while. Two women walked down the path along the riverbank. They were probably going to visit the shrine. "I feel something is watching us. Watching and stalking, like a sea serpent under the surface of the sea, stalking a ship that does not know the danger it's in."

CHAPTER 13

THE THUNDER rolled in not much later, and Johanna went down into the hold. Nellie brought dinner and Johanna stood patiently for Nellie to take more measurements, while the rain pelted on the hold covers. Loesie had made good progress on the lace and declared that the dress would be ready on time.

Johanna was just getting dressed again when there were footsteps and the sound of voices from outside.

She went to look. The brief shower had come and gone. Julianna Nieland was on the jetty in the presence of a group of children.

"There she is!" one of them yelled.

Another one called out, "Can His Royal Majesty please come outside? We want to catch frogs."

Julianna pulled a face. "They've been spending too much time inside with all this rain. They've been driving us all crazy."

Roald must have heard the word "frogs" because he came to the top of the stairs carrying his net, to much cheering from the children.

He led the group of boys into the reed bed with much chattering and excitement, in which terms of *Your Majesty* were often forgotten.

Julianna smiled. "They love him so much and he's so good with them."

He deserved a family of his own, and that brought Johanna back to the painful thought that this was not happening.

Julianna said, "I really came here because you had a council meeting this morning and I was wondering if Shepherd Carolus had said something to you about going somewhere. He was meant to come and teach the kids, but he didn't show up. He's often late, but he always comes."

Johanna's heart skipped a beat. "He wasn't at the council meeting either. Master Deim went out to find him but he couldn't. Someone seemed to think that he'd gone to harvest."

"In the rain?"

They looked at each other. An expression of worry hovered in Julianna's eyes. There was no need for words. They both thought the same thing: something has happened to him.

"Pieter!" Johanna called out to the guards at the jetty.

The man on question turned.

"Have you seen Shepherd Carolus at all today?"

"Yes, I remember seeing him—no, I remember wrongly. That was yesterday."

"He was meant to come to the council meeting, but he wasn't there. He was meant to teach the children, but he didn't show up. That's not like him at all. Could you check his tent? In fact, I'll come with you."

Pieter accompanied Johanna across the camp. Shepherd Carolus didn't have any relatives in the camp, and shared with a group of single men. None of them had seen him.

A young nobleman's son said, "I thought it was funny that I got up early this morning, and it didn't look like he'd been there all night. You know that we keep quiet about that sort of thing, and I thought it was a bit strange, him being a priest and all that, but you know . . ." He shrugged. His cheeks turned red. "I'm sorry, this is not an appropriate subject for a lady."

Well, thank you for thinking so much of him. "Why didn't you say anything earlier?"

"Because he's often away. He does a lot of things."

"He'll be all right," another man said. "Likely, he got so smitten with a girl from town that he's still with her. He's a big and handsome fellow."

"But not turning up for teaching a class?"

"A bit odd, I have to confess." He looked uneasy. "Although he did say something about going into town for shoes for children."

"Have you seen anything unusual?"

"No. I don't think so." But something made him hesitant.

"Would you help me check around the camp just to make sure?"

Master Deim came as well, and they walked over the road at the back of the camp and then up and down the river bank several times, past the reed beds and the little shrine that stood further from the bank than it had been when it was erected. They went as far as the boat shed and then back in the other direction. In places, the path had been claimed by the rising waters and they had to walk through the tall grass.

There was no sign of Shepherd Carolus, no sign that someone had been this way.

"He probably just went into town and got held up," Pieter said.

Johanna met Master Deim's eyes. It was probably not wise to say anything about magic in Pieter's presence. He would only report it to the nobles and they would use it against her at the next meeting.

They checked the shed, the reeds and the river. If Shepherd Carolus had gone to town, he would have come this way.

But there was no one on the path. The vast churning surface of the water remained empty. The riverbanks were deserted, the tall grass undisturbed.

With the low clouds, it started to go dark quite soon and veils of mist rose from the water.

"We better go back," Master Deim said. "He's obviously not here."

"I'll go and ask in town tomorrow," Pieter said. "If he hasn't returned by then. But he will probably turn up soon."

Johanna wished she could believe that, but the cold fingers of magic were reaching for her again. She brushed her hands over a few tree trunks while they walked, but they showed her nothing significant, except ducks. One showed the two scouts setting off in their dinghy towards Saardam.

They haven't returned either.

Shapes swirled in the mist but every time she thought she saw ghosts in the corner of her eye, they disappeared again once she turned her head to look in more detail.

Yet, there was *something*. Watching, waiting.

Johanna shivered.

When they came back to the *Lady Sara* it was dusk. Loesie and Nellie stood on the jetty, talking to Captain Arense.

"There they are!" Nellie called out. She came towards the shore. "Oh, mistress Johanna, we were so worried about you!"

But it was Loesie who drew Johanna's attention. She was sitting on the hold covers, her arms around her legs which she held drawn up to her chest. Her eyes were vacant.

"What happened?"

"There were ghosts," Nellie said. "In the reeds over there." She pointed.

"Did Roald see them?" That was where he had been looking for frogs.

"I don't think so. The children had already gone. We were looking for you because we didn't know where you were. We worried that you'd fallen off the deck and no one had noticed. Loesie saw the ghost first. She's been sitting like this since then. It's like she went back to being bewitched. I'm afraid, Mistress Johanna."

Johanna climbed the gangplank and joined Loesie on the hold covers. Loesie was shivering and muttering to herself.

"What did you see?" Johanna asked.

"Must not talk to it. Must not look at it. Must not talk to it. Must not look at it." Loesie stared into nothingness.

"Not talk to what?"

"Must not talk to it. Must not look at it."

"Loesie?"

Loesie faced her. Her eyes were still alert, too alert for her to have become possessed again.

"What did you see? A ghost?"

"Must not talk to it. Must not look at it."

"Loesie, answer me."

Loesie screamed and clamped her hands over her ears. "Don't talk to it! Don't! Don't! Leave me alone. Push me in the river. Put me in a boat without oars. Let me go, please!"

"What are you talking about?"

"Get away from me!"

Johanna slid back off the hold cover. Loesie went back to her previous position, with her arms wrapped around her legs. No amount of coaxing could bring her down.

"I don't understand," Nellie said. "She was doing so well."

"I don't think she was ever completely cured from that demon," Johanna said. "She never went back to the way she used to be. I'm sure you remember that she always spoke with a strong dialect and that she always used magic to scare boys in the marketplace."

"Yes, I do remember. Thankfully, she stopped that."

"It's not as simple as that. You can't just learn to speak differently overnight. The demon changed her personality. It's still changing her."

That brought a chill and neither of them said anything for a while.

"What can we do about it?" Nellie finally said in a low voice.

"Nothing. Wait until she calms down. Go to your cabin. Maybe she'll be fine once we stop fussing over her. There is not much point in arguing with her in this state."

Nellie turned, and then looked over her shoulder.

"Mistress Johanna, do you think she could be dangerous?"

"I don't know, Nellie. I really don't know."

Johanna felt guilty letting Nellie go back to the cabin alone. Maybe she would have to let Nellie sleep in the hold away from Loesie, but that would mean that she and Roald would lose whatever privacy they had. Somehow, that suddenly seemed important, that little home they had made for themselves.

She descended the stairs in that familiar, somewhat musty, smell of the hold. Roald sat at his desk, drawing a frog which he had caught in a glass jar. The drawing was so beautiful and detailed that she forgot all her objections about *no frogs in our bedroom*.

Roald was pleased that she liked it and from one thing came another. They moved from the desk to the bed. With all the worry about Shepherd Carolus and Loesie, she didn't care about doing it the right way, and she sat on him because she much preferred it this way. And something else happened that she had not experienced before. A lot of the time when she was with Roald, she would feel that there ought to be more to it, and that it seemed unfair that just he found it pleasurable. In fact, some of the books suggested that the woman should find pleasure, too. That experience of intimate pleasure crept up on her unnoticed, grabbed hold of her and took her so much by surprise that she cried out, perhaps a bit too loud. Roald thought it was so interesting that he probed her soft flesh with his fingers until it happened again, and then he wanted to do it a third time, but she was a bit sore and tired, and there was sticky seed everywhere.

Tomorrow, she said, and he was happy with that.

Before drifting off to sleep, she realised that she had forgotten to drink the raspberry leaf tea.

CHAPTER 14

JOHANNA WAS WAKENED by rustling noises in the hold. They'd had mice in the room before, but this sounded bigger and too close for comfort. She got out of bed and found that last night they had forgotten that the frog still sat in the glass jar. During the darkest part of the night, it obviously remained quiet, but now it was rustling around in the leaves, trying to climb out of the jar. Poor thing.

Much as she disliked frogs, and she disliked them less since Roald had explained all about their strange life cycles, she didn't think it would be very happy in the jar, so she took the jar up to the deck of the ship—

And found that the morning dawned with mist rising out of the river. The sky above was pale blue, but all around, mist shrouded the land.

A bite to the air heralded the coming of autumn. The guards stood huddled in their cloaks. Loesie had evidently decided to go to bed well before midnight, because the hold cover was empty and the dew had coated the timber covers evenly with no trace that anyone had been there recently.

Johanna went down the gangplank carrying the jar. The guards gave her strange looks but said nothing.

She waded through the tall grass to the water and upended the jar. With a giant leap, the frog went *splash* into the water, leaving ripples as it went below the surface.

She was about to turn back and ask the guards if by chance they had heard whether Shepherd Carolus had returned when there were alarmed voices from further downstream.

Johanna's heart beat faster. That was coming from the direction of the shrine. The apparition of Celine hadn't shown itself since that day the boys had seen her. Johanna had hoped that it had been a one-time appearance, some magician's idea of a joke, but had always known that hope was for fools.

Johanna made her way around the reed bed walking as fast as she could without running.

A number of people stood there, staring at the water. People shrank back to make a wide path to let Johanna through to the water's edge. They said nothing. Mothers pulled children out of her path.

The platform on top of the post had been smashed; the flowers and the little crude statue were gone. Scraps of wood lay between the reeds along the swollen river. Someone had stomped all over the offerings laid out on the riverbank. Big, booted footsteps over crushed flowers.

"Does anyone know who did this?" Johanna asked.

Fearful silence was her only response, a crowd of pale faces and wide eyes.

After a while, a little boy said, "This is how we found it this morning."

His mother shushed him.

"Did anyone see people here?"

Now another boy said, "We were out playing this morning, and we saw no one." This boy's mother tried to shush him, too, but he turned to her and said, loud enough for Johanna to hear, "What? I'm telling the truth. We saw no one."

Johanna addressed the adults. "What is going on here? Do any of you know who did this?"

People shook their heads, but no one said anything.

"Wait. Does anyone think I did this?"

There were some more shakes of heads, most not very convincing. Some people looked away.

A woman fell to her knees in the grass.

"Celine! Speak to us! This is not our fault. Please forgive us."

Another was crying as well, wailing like a young child.

These were nobles, people who normally prided themselves on being business-like, sensible people who tut-tutted if someone displayed overt emotions. The same people who had ridiculed King Nicholaos for being incapacitated with grief at his daughter's funeral.

"I assure you that I had nothing to do with this act of destruction. I will do everything I can to find out who did this."

The looks that met hers seemed to be of pity more than anger.

Wait—had someone destroyed the shrine because they wanted to make her unpopular? She knew who might do something like that.

Johanna hurried along the riverbank to the camp. She had enough and was going to get to the bottom of this despicable act.

Ignatius Hemeldinck stayed with the family of Johan Delacoeur. They were well-prepared, with sturdy tents. This part of the camp was also higher up the riverbank and not as muddy as the lower areas. Again, the men of power looked after themselves well enough. Never mind the sick and very young people, and the school, where Julianna worked in a tent where the floor consisted of muddy straw.

She ran up to the tent and announced herself with a loud, "Hullo!" as she would normally do when visiting warehouses for her Father. She had not come here to be polite.

An old man pushed the tent flap aside.

"I'd like to speak to Ignatius Hemeldinck."

"Wait here, missy."

He let the fabric drop.

Missy? She was married to their legal king. What did he think he was that he could call her that? In fact, what did all of these pompous idiots think they were doing?

The sound of male voices came from inside the tent and not much later the man himself pushed the tent flap aside.

His eyebrows rose.

Johanna launched straight into the problem. "This morning the shrine to Celine was destroyed." Johanna had to do her best to keep her tone civilised.

He gave her a *yes, and?* look.

"Do you know who was involved?"

"Pray, why should I know?" In that usual *dumb woman* tone of his. "Ask some of those ratbag boys. They probably know more."

"You wouldn't happen to have told them to destroy it?"

"Why should I do that?" He half-turned, as if the conversation was over, as if she wasn't worth his time, and to be honest, that was probably what he thought about her all along.

"I will explain it to you." Now she definitely let her anger colour her voice.

He gave her a mildly surprised look.

"You may not remember it, but you said you wanted the shrine taken away when it first went up. You wanted to, in your own words, *remove the whole damn thing overnight* and you didn't seem to care much about what the people would have to say about that, because *they were only women*."

"For a merchant girl, you're starting to become incredibly irritating."

That was it. She was through with the lot of them. "I do not appreciate talk like that. I'm still married to your rightful king, and I'm starting to think you are setting up a plot against my husband. Maybe all of this is part of that plan. Engaging your magic friends to create ghosts that look like Celine—"

He opened his mouth—

"No, don't tell me that there isn't any magic. This place is stiff with magic. This town is full of magicians. Don't blame me for destroying the shrine. Don't address me like I'm your daughter because I am not." She hated this man so much. Him, and Fleuris LaFontaine and Octavio Nieland who was said to have joined the occupiers. These were not men who cared for the citizens of Saardam. They didn't even care about their families. These men only cared about themselves.

He looked taken aback, a puzzled frown on his face.

Johanna went on, "Next time we have a council meeting, you will apologise to Roald for the things you said about him."

"Do stop making such a spectacle of yourself. Look at it, everyone has come out to watch." Indeed, a lot of people had come out of the surrounding tents.

"So, I am 'making a spectacle of myself' when I protest about you constantly ignoring me, belittling me and acting as if I'm stupid. I've had enough of this behaviour. I will not be talked down to! You will either listen to me or Roald, or I will no longer consider you loyal to the royal family."

He laughed, but his expression was uneasy. He glanced around at all the onlookers, meeting the eyes of one group behind Johanna in particular. Johanna glanced over her shoulder. Julianna Nieland stood there with Captain Arense's wife and three sons.

Ignatius bowed, equally uneasy. "As you wish, lady."

"Your Majesty." Johanna disliked pomp, but it seemed the only thing that would impress these men.

"Your Majesty." It sounded like his words came through gritted teeth.

Good. There would probably be trouble about this later, but she had tried being friendly with them, and it had failed.

"I shall now call a meeting of the council. I will inform you what we are going to do to return to Saardam, to reinstate Roald in the palace, to rebuild the palace, and drive the invaders out. You are free to advise us. Unless you wish me to go ahead with my plans without informing you."

Johanna whirled around and met the eyes of a bunch of women standing in the entrance to the next tent. She didn't know them by name, but they were all smiling. Oh yes, there was support for her in the camp. The women, the quiet and civilised men, the merchants. She just needed to give these people the courage to act.

Not much later, the Council of Nobles convened in the boat shed. It was not their usual meeting time, and Fleuris LaFontaine had to be hunted down from some place in town. He came into the boat shed muttering and protesting and sat down at the table with a heavy sigh.

His face was red from the wine he had evidently consumed with his midday meal.

Johanna had thought it wise to let Roald stay at the *Lady Sara*. He'd been teaching some boys how to catch butterflies without damaging them, and had gotten wet. He had sticks in his hair and smudges on his cheeks and, when she called, had looked at her with such disappointment that she couldn't bring herself to drag him along to a meeting, let alone one where tempers were sure to get heated. He hated it when people raised their voices, because he didn't understand that they weren't talking to him. He might start fidgeting, laughing or screaming, and that would be unacceptable.

So she had watched him trundle back into the reeds with his butterfly net, wishing she could be with him. Instead, she had changed into in her best dress, put on the necklace, brooch and earrings that she had brought from Duke Lothar's castle—much as she hated wearing other people's property—and then went to look for Nellie to put up her hair.

She couldn't find Nellie or Loesie and concluded that they were probably looking after the laundry, so she did her own hair and asked her guard escorts to walk her to the boat shed. Johanna was nervous and her insides squirmed, giving her cramps in her stomach. She took up the position at the head of the table that would normally be Roald's.

Johan Delacoeur gave her a look icy enough to make water freeze. He was a powerful man, an ex-army general with connections in armies all around the low lands. In their return to Saardam, he would be an asset, if she could win his support, no matter how reluctantly given. If.

Master Deim smiled at her from the other end of the table, which made her feel a bit more confident. Shepherd Carolus was still absent, reminding her of another painful problem that needed to be solved. That meant that she was down two supporters in the council.

Now that she'd called this meeting, there was no going back, so she might as well jump in before she lost control of the moment.

"I've called you here, because I want to ascertain your loyalty. I want all of you to swear loyalty to the royal family. When that is done, I want your honesty about your plans for the future of all those camping in this field. We cannot stay here over winter and I want to return to Saardam with whoever will come."

Fleuris made scoffing noises. "Well, I don't know that it's safe—"

"Staying here is safe? Where every time it rains, water rises into the lower areas of the camp, bringing filth and disease? Where our citizens are assailed by magic, seeing ghosts, being struck with apathy? I know that many of you are not aware of this, but this town soaks in magic, and someone or something is waiting to pounce on us. Whoever it is, they know who we are. They know about Roald. But every time I've raised the issue of returning home, you have tried to push it aside, tried to ignore or deflect it—"

Fleuris LaFontaine said, "If you want the truth of it, Alexandre uses filthy magic, that's why."

"Then why haven't you tried to find a magician to deal with him for us?"

He snorted.

"All of the courts around here have magicians." She looked around the table, meeting a collection of hard stares.

"I will tell you why. Because some of you have made a deal with the Baron. You didn't like the influence the Church of the Triune was having on the people and on your royal family. Some time long before the fire, some of you came here to ask for help, where you have friends, and the Baron suggested that he knew a way to get rid of this church for you. He sent Alexandre Trebuchet who adores the Baron so much that he'd eat dirt if the Baron asked him. But things got very much out of hand for you, because I doubt you knew about fire magic, and I doubt you asked for the whole of Saardam to be set on fire, but you could not control or stop him, especially since some of your peers joined Alexandre. So you came here because your main reason was to complain to the Baron. He has allowed you to camp in this field and made you feel important and welcome, but now he won't listen to you anymore, because you served his purpose."

There were several gasps around the table.

At the same time Johan shouted, "Nonsense!" Fleuris shouted, "And what purpose would that be?"

Ignatius said nothing and looked distinctly uncomfortable and Master Deim's eyes were so big that they were in danger of tumbling from their sockets.

All of which told her that she was right about all her assumptions.

Johanna remained quiet and let the men rage.

While Johan heaped protest on protest, going *Whatever do you think you are?* and *Do you know what the Baron has done for us?* and *You have no right to be so ungrateful to our best friend,* Fleuris fell silent and eventually Johan ran out of protests to hurl at her. He crossed his arms over his chest and breathed through flaring nostrils. His face had gone red.

Because I'm right, and he doesn't like the way the Baron ignores him either.

When the nobles had fallen into an angry silence, she said, "There are a number of things we can do."

Captain Arense rarely spoke in these meetings, but he said, "Have you talked to the Baron?" His soft and civilised voice made everyone look at him.

"I have tried to. I have spoken to the Baroness several times, but I don't think there is a point in talking to the Baron. Even if we manage to get an audience, he will continue to ignore us. He clearly thinks that he has better things to do than listen to our complaints. We don't need him to return to our own city."

They didn't even need the Baroness' help in organising the wedding. They didn't need the Baron's prying guests at what was a Saarlander ceremony.

"We need an army," Mayor Joris DeCamp said.

Johan Delacoeur snorted.

Johanna said, "I'm not even sure that an army would do much good against magic." They needed stealth. They needed to disguise themselves as peasants. They needed to come into the city one by one, like farmers going to the markets. Loesie could help with that. They also needed magicians.

"I said several times that going back is ridiculous," Fleuris said. "I'll say it again. I, for one, am not going to take your accusations lightly. You accuse us of disloyalty—"

"This is why I called the meeting. I want to know where you stand: with the Baron or us."

Fleuris spread his hands. "By the heavens, woman, why don't you see that the Baron is on our side?"

"Then why won't he talk to any of us?"

"He doesn't talk to women."

"He's not talking to you either."

"What do you know about the meetings we've had with him? He has assured us that he is on our side." He crossed his arms over his chest.

"If you're so friendly with the Baron then, I ask that you go and talk to him and ask him for assistance to return to Saardam. Because certainly, you agree we can't stay here for the winter in this wet field, and I don't think Florisheim has enough spare houses for us."

He harrumphed. "All right."

"We will meet again here next week and you'll report what the Baron said."

He glanced aside to Johan, whose face was impassive, and then to Ignatius, who looked like he wanted to have her for dinner. Neither said anything.

He said again, "All right. I make no promises." Because he could make no promises, because the Baron wasn't even in town. For all she knew, the Baron was in the palace in Saardam with Alexandre.

"I happen to think that the people of Saardam are owed some promises. They are also owed an explanation of who you think the enemy is and why exactly a foreign magician was given the opportunity, encouragement even, to burn much of our home town."

He gave her a hard stare.

"Also, I want someone to find out who destroyed the shrine to Celine. Like you, I am unhappy about its existence, but there is no need to disturb the people further. We will also contact anyone who can shed light on the appearance of this ghost, and will talk to people who may know about King Nicholaos' involvement in dark magic. The Magician's Guild in Florisheim will probably know more about Alexandre Trebuchet and his masters."

They looked uneasy, but Johanna had enough of being dictated by these men only to be waiting for things they said they'd do but never did. She'd probably made a number of enemies, but they were never going to be friends in the first place.

She was fully prepared to go to the Magician's Guild herself, but at least she had notified them about her intentions and reasons for doing so.

They broke up the meeting, and one or two people actually called her *Your Majesty*. Not any of the nobles, though. But they had stopped calling her *just a merchant girl*. That was progress of a kind.

The meeting broke up and Johanna left the shed with Master Deim.

"I don't like the thought of asking for magical assistance," he said, while walking along the riverbank.

"I wish we could get by without it, too, but we have little choice. We have to act. I hate just sitting here and waiting for something to happen. I wanted to train Loesie as court magician, but she doesn't want to have anything to do with magic. I think we *need* a court magician, or someone to advise us on the subject of magic," she added, after remembering what Magda had said about court magicians being jesters.

He nodded again. "Yes, probably."

"Where would I find a person like that? I thought you were going to make some inquiries?"

"I was, but—"

But what he was going to say would have to wait, because a young boy came running up the path. "Look, look, Your Majesty, what I've found. Mother said to show it to you."

From his fist dangled a golden chain on which hung the medallion with the symbol of the Triune. The last time she had seen this it was on Shepherd Carolus' neck.

Johanna took it from him. The chain had broken and parts of the medallion were covered in dark mud.

"Where did you find this?"

"In the grass on the edge of the forest."

Johanna's heart jumped. "Can you show me?"

CHAPTER 15

JOHANNA AND Master Deim followed the boy, and one of Johan Delacoeur's guards came as well. As they crossed the camp, several people noticed that something was going on and they followed at a distance.

The boy's name was Gijsbert, and he was the son of one of the merchants in the camp. While he led them across the camp, across the road on the other side and down a narrow track towards the forest, he chatted incessantly about how he and his friends had been playing on the haystack when he found the Shepherd's medallion. Of the Shepherd himself, he had seen no trace.

Squalls of wind made Johanna shiver, even though it was quite warm. Master Deim looked uneasy, too.

The path ran between two paddocks. One contained a couple of horses that were trotting around tossing their heads and with their tails held up so that the soft part of the tail flowed behind like a banner.

"What are those crazy horses doing?" the guard muttered behind Johanna.

But she knew what disturbed the animals: they were much more sensitive to magic than people.

The dark forest loomed at the far end of those paddocks, mostly oaks trees with dense foliage and dark canopies.

The sun chose that time to disappear behind the building clouds. A gust of wind made the leaves rustle in soft whispers. Ghosts waited in that forest. Waited and prowled, ready to pounce on anyone who dared step into their domain.

Gijsbert ran ahead.

Johanna fought the urge to yell at him to come back, to stay with the rest of the group. What business did Shepherd Carolus have in that forest anyway?

At the boundary between the field and the forest stood a wooden barn with one open side. A multitude of cart tracks led through and around the puddles in front of it. This appeared to be where a lot of the hay and straw had come from.

"This is where I found it," the boy said, pointing at the ground.

There was nothing much to be seen except mud and tracks: deep ruts from wagon wheels and churned-up mud from horse hooves.

Everyone in the group walked around for a bit, examining the ground.

"This is the most recent one," the guard said, kneeling. He pointed at a set of tracks that led not back to the road, but into the forest.

The forest that surrounded the group on three sides was full of whispering leaves. The sky had gone leaden grey over the tree line.

Slowly, Johanna walked to the closest tree. She put her hand on the trunk.

The gloominess in the forest disappeared and was replaced with dappled sunlight falling through the trees.

There was the clop-clop-clop of horse's hooves and a cart came past. The driver wore a dark brown cloak with the hood draped over his shoulders. He had an unusually heavy brow and his dark hair fell loose over his shoulders. The man next to him was Shepherd Carolus. As the cart passed, the Shepherd looked over his shoulder directly at the tree, as if he knew that Johanna could see him. He moved his mouth like a fish on land, but Johanna couldn't make out words.

The driver flicked the reins and the horse took off. The back of the driver's hood had an embroidered symbol that she hadn't seen before: a yellow key.

The Baroness Viktoriya sat down on the couch with a sigh. She had accompanied Johanna to a garden room with doors and windows along one side. The flowers in the castle garden outside looked bedraggled from the rain.

"Unfortunately, my husband is not at home, so I will help you, right?"

She was wearing a dark green dress today and a black vest, a sombre ensemble without lace, which, apart from the rather low neckline, would not look out of place in church in Saardam. The only spot of brightness was a gold and jade brooch that held her shawl in place. Her dark hair was piled on top of her head, held in place by a hair net with tiny glass beads.

They were both silent while a maid brought some tea and a plate with dainty little cakes. She set a cup on a little table next to Johanna. The brew was dark and smelled sweet.

"Thank you for seeing me," Johanna said. "I'm sorry for imposing on your time."

"Oh, don't be so modest. Of course I make time to help my friend. Do help yourself to some cakes."

"But you're obviously busy." She wasn't too sure that she'd

call the Baroness a friend either. But she did take a cake from the plate.

"Pfa." The Baroness flapped her hand. "Busy, busy. It's always busy. My husband spend so much time away lately, is getting really tiresome. So much work to be done! Harvest fields, sell geldings, move cattle . . . is all boring. I have to check, check, check all the time that everything gets done. Then it rain, rain and rain and people have to check the water mills and take hay to other barn, and . . ." She sighed heavily. "And my son is no help. I don't even know where he is. Gallivanting with his friends from across river, I guess, but I wish he grow up. I want a woman in family. That's why I invite your wedding at castle. I get best cooks. Hans Salter and his music troupe will play. There will be much dancing. I have big feast so my son will see what a wedding is like. Maybe he get jealous, he wants a wedding, too."

Knowing what she knew about Kylian, she doubted it.

"I'm sure you're doing your best, and thank you so much." And now she felt guilty for not wanting the festivities in the Baron's big hall. The Baroness was doing a lot of work for this ceremony, and obviously, she led a very lonely life.

A young man in the Baron's red livery came into the room, but stopped when he saw Johanna.

He said something and the Baroness replied, her tone somewhat annoyed. Then he bowed and left the room.

"I see you're busy," Johanna said. "I won't take much of your time. In all truth, I didn't come here to talk about the wedding."

"Oh?" The delicately painted eyebrows went up. "I like talking about wedding. We must talk about guests. I've made a long list of people to invite."

Johanna had been afraid of that. "I'm very sorry to have to mention this to you, but one of our people went missing from the camp yesterday. I was wondering if you could offer any assistance in finding him."

"How dreadful. What happened?"

Johanna told her of the Shepherd's absence and the chain they had found and the fact that he had been taken away in a cart. She described the cart driver's cloak and the symbol of the key on the back of the hood. She had drawn it on a piece of paper that she had taken from Roald's desk.

While she spoke, the Baroness' eyes widened. "But that is just awful. If my husband was here, he'd come and help you find this man personally and punish those who abducted him."

"Do you know which group uses this symbol?" Johanna held up the paper.

The Baroness squinted at it. "No. Have not seen that before."

"I'd be happy if you could lend me some people to help us ask around in town." A group of men had gone into town that morning, but had not found any sign of the Shepherd, nor of the shoemaker he was supposed to have gone to see. But they'd run into trouble because some of the townsfolk were suspicious about their presence, which was why she needed the Baroness' help.

"I will send some men, definitely. I'll see to it as soon as you leave this room. They will go through entire town and will not leave a house unvisited. They will find this man."

"Thank you so much." Johanna would have preferred if the Baroness just lent her someone who could explain to the townsfolk who they were looking for, but she guessed it would be impolite to complain.

So she drank tea and listened to the Baroness' plans for the wedding. Both the tea and cakes were really sweet to the point of making her feel a bit queasy. This room was strangely luxurious compared to the austerity of the rest of the castle and a world away from her little room in the *Lady Sara*'s hold.

They discussed dresses and food and guests, most of whom Johanna didn't know. She didn't want to ask if Duke Lothar and his son would be there, but she guessed not if history was anything to go by. She wanted to go back to the camp, but didn't want to be rude. The Baroness just kept talking and talking and didn't give Johanna an opportunity to leave. The wooden armrests of her chair told her that noble townsfolk visited this room often and that there would be much tea and chatter, all in the dialect, sadly, so Johanna had no idea what they talked about. Meanwhile she still tried to steer the discussion to more useful subjects.

"I'm a bit worried about what happens *after* the wedding. Because much as we appreciate your hospitality, winter is coming and we need more permanent quarters—"

"Oh, but you can stay longer. Plenty of room for you in castle."

"Thank you very much, but I would prefer to return home. Maybe some people would like to make further use of your hospitality, but many of us have family in Saardam that we're worried about. We should return home. I and my husband should return."

"I understand." She gave Johanna a sympathetic look, but said nothing further.

"But I don't want to return to a dangerous situation. Do you have any more news from Saardam?"

"No more than what you already know. It will be dangerous to go there, I'd say."

"We sent some scouts to see for ourselves what was going on, but they haven't yet returned. Has your husband said anything about what is going on there?"

"Dear, my husband is barely ever home, and he does not talk about politics to me. He knows I'm not interested."

"Do you know Alexandre?" Johanna promised herself that she would never be one of those women "not interested" in the dealings of men with power.

"He is a most snivelling man," the Baroness said. "I like him not at all." She wrinkled her nose as if an unpleasant smell wafted past.

"Does your husband like him?"

She laughed. "What do you think? That he would make serious discussions with this little man?"

"He has rather a lot of magic."

"Bah, it's fire magic—all spectacle."

"To the citizens of Saardam, it certainly wasn't just a spectacle." Johanna couldn't help letting some anger seep into her voice.

"I do apologise. It was terrible for you. But fire magic is nothing. Not important. Setting fire to a city, it is what cowards do. I could do it. He think he is important, but he is not."

"He seems to think a lot of your husband."

"Yes, but only because he is a snivelling little man. I said to my husband many times to shut him up. Not to listen to him. This man is up to no good, I'd say, but my husband, he is stubborn. One day, this priest might be useful, he'd say. So he invite Alexandre here, in our own castle. And I have to make talk with him, and be polite to him while he behave like a drunk ship's boy."

Johanna had visions of rowdy fests in the big hall with its many long tables and benches. A Shepherd of the Church of the Triune would never come to an occasion like that. The church abhorred overt displays of wealth. Shepherds dressed plainly. The citizens coming to church dressed in their best clothes that were still modest.

"And he is a dirty little man, too. I wanted to slap him in the face all the time he tries to put his hands up my dress."

She felt a jab of sympathy for the Baroness. "Oh dear, that sounds awful."

"Nothing as awful as what happened to you, but yes, it was quite dreadful."

"Why do you think he went to Saardam?"

The Baroness spread her hands. "If we knew, it would be the end of troubles. Maybe he want money. Maybe he want blond-haired girls. Maybe he want ships. I don't know." The baroness sighed. "Let's leave that for the men to solve. One more thing about the wedding. I would like the Holy Father Lucius to conduct the ceremony, but I don't think you are baptised."

"No." There was a small Belaman Church building in Saardam, if it was still there, but Johanna didn't know many people who attended services there. Mistress Daphne was one, and a few other foreigners.

"You would need to become a member of the church."

No way. Just no way. If there was to be a ceremony, Shepherd Carolus would conduct it—after they found out where he was. "But I think I am already a member of your church? Aren't we all part of the same church?"

The Baroness gave her a sharp look. "My dear, you haven't heard?"

"Heard what?"

The Baroness raised her hand to her mouth. "You really haven't heard about the Most Holy Father's decree?"

"No, I don't think so." That would be the Most Holy Father Severino of the Belaman Church.

"Well . . . he decreed that there were . . . differences between the holy scriptures as understood by us and as interpreted by your Shepherd. Differences that needed . . . investigation." She frowned and then her expression cleared. "An inquisition. That's it. And he had the results of the inquisition."

"And that means?"

"I don't know how to say precisely in words of the church, but it means that the Church founded by Brother Romulus is no longer welcome as part of the Belaman Church."

CHAPTER 16

IN ONE HIT, Johanna finally understood the cause of all the problems. While Saardam had fallen under the Belaman Church, the church fathers had thought of the Shepherd Romulus as an eccentric. Now that it was no longer part of the Belaman Church, the Church of the Triune was a threat. The Shepherds were a threat. They helped common people who ended up liking the Shepherds for that reason. They won the respect of citizens that way. All the citizens, not just the nobles who could buy sympathy from the church. They did not insist on donations by the wealthy, who expected special services in return, and did not flaunt wealth. And that frightened the leadership of the Belaman Church, because there were so many more common people than there were nobles.

And with that thought, she became very concerned for Shepherd Carolus' safety.

She had no idea how she managed to get out of the room without promising anything, but one thing she knew: they needed to get out of here as soon as possible. And find Shepherd Carolus, *without* help from the Baroness' men. If the

Belaman Church was behind the abduction, then the conflict stepped up a whole new level, and all their lives were in danger, unless they converted.

Johanna hurried through the streets of the town back to the *Lady Sara*, but when she arrived there, only Roald was home, seated at the desk, reading.

She noticed wet footsteps on the stairs. "Your shoes are wet."

He didn't react. Johanna dumped the drawing of the key symbol on the desk and kneeled at his feet. His shoes were indeed wet and covered in duckweed. "Let me take them off, then I'll put them outside to dry."

She wriggled his shoes off his feet. His socks were wet, too—and very smelly—and his toes had gone wrinkled like dried gooseberries. Phew, the smell was strong.

"Do you know where Nellie is?" She didn't hold much hope for a reply.

"There was some . . . thing going on."

Her heart jumped. "What sort of thing?"

"They were making a lot of noise up there. I told them to be quiet."

"Who is 'they'?"

He shrugged and went back to his book.

Johanna climbed back to the deck and went into the cabin to look for signs of where Nellie and Loesie were. Just then, Nellie was coming towards the jetty carrying a basket from which carrot greens protruded.

"Oh, mistress Johanna. You're back." The tone in her voice didn't sound happy.

"Yes. Roald said that there had been noise on the deck. What happened?"

"It was not my fault."

"What happened, Nellie?"

"I swear it wasn't my fault, mistress Johanna. Don't be angry with me."

"Just tell me what happened."

Nellie led Johanna back up the gangplank. In the cabin, she took a basket that stood on the bed which contained the dress she had been making. She lifted it out of the basket and the bottom of it was torn to shreds as if a wild animal had taken to it.

Nellie's eyes brimmed over with tears, her hands trembled so much that she could barely hold the dress up. "I didn't do it."

"I believe you, Nellie. Do you know who did?" But she already knew the answer before Nellie told her.

"That witch. She was sitting on the floor and poking a knife through the fabric and then tearing it."

"Loesie?"

Nellie nodded, sniffing. "I really thought she was getting better, mistress Johanna. Learning how to sew and cook. I'm so sorry for trusting her. It's my fault that you won't have a pretty dress—"

"Nellie, stop it." Johanna prised the dress from Nellie's hands. "I like a pretty dress, but it's not so important that I want you to—"

"But what about the wedding?"

"If things keep up like this, there won't be one until we're back in Saardam, and when we are, I'd be happy to get married in this dress. It is not important. Where is Loesie now?"

"I don't know. I told her to get off the ship. I wasn't very nice about it, mistress Johanna. I'm sorry." Her chin trembled.

"It's all right, Nellie. I probably would have done the same. But we do need to find her, before anything really bad happens."

Nellie nodded, her eyes wide. "Someone needs to look after her. I have to apologise."

"Whatever for?"

"I might have used some bad words. I was very upset when I saw her sitting there destroying the dress. But she is obviously not in her right mind. No healthy person would do that."

"I have to find her." With dread, she also realised that Loesie was probably responsible for the destruction of the shrine, and whatever still ailed her was buried deep in her soul.

Johanna walked through the entire camp a number of times, but didn't see Loesie anywhere. She asked everyone she met, but none of those people had seen her either. She ran into Master Deim, and together they widened the search to the surrounding fields and reed beds. They didn't find her on the riverbank to the south of the camp or anywhere near the boatshed. They didn't find her on the main road into town or in the fields on the other side. The horses that grazed there came to the fence and walked with them to the hay shed where Shepherd Carolus had disappeared. There was no magic to upset them today, and Johanna knew they weren't going to find Loesie at the shed long before they got there. Indeed they didn't.

They returned to the main road and walked north of the camp. This was an area even more marshy than the part of the riverbank between the camp and the boat shed.

The water had invaded low-lying stands of willow trees, which now stood with their trunks in the water. Most of the trees were saplings and they grew very close together. Branches had fallen haphazardly in between the trees and reeds and vines had grown over the dead wood, turning the area into an impenetrable thicket. The occasional bramble bush didn't help either.

Johanna and Master Deim walked along the narrow path that ran halfway up a row of hillocks, peering into the vegetation tangle.

If Loesie had gone in there, they had no hope of finding her. In the water, she wouldn't even have left tracks.

"We're not going to find her here," Master Deim said. "Would she have gone into town?"

"Unlikely. Loesie doesn't like people. Not unless someone forced her." And that was a thought she didn't want to entertain at this point. Although the demon likely belonged to someone and that someone would come for it at some point. This place was stiff with magic and if there was a magician tied to Loesie's demon, that magician might well live in Florisheim.

Johanna heard Magda's voice talking about *the betrayer*. She might well have been talking about Loesie. Since Loesie had been with the group from the beginning, she might have been like a burning beacon of magic to those who could see it, letting everyone know where they were all the time.

Johanna's chest constricted with panic. She didn't watch where she put her feet and tripped over a branch. She fell on her hands and knees.

Master Deim rushed to her. "My child! Are you all right?"

"I think so." Johanna brushed mud from her hands and dress. It would need to be washed once again.

"Let's go back. We're not going to find her here."

"Maybe we should try going to town, unlikely as it sounds."

But as she pushed herself up, she caught a glimpse of fabric between the trees ahead. She pointed. "There."

Master Deim peered into the thicket. "I do believe you're right."

He pushed a couple of branches aside. "There is a path of sorts here."

Path was a big word for the animal track that led over the faintest rise between close growing willow saplings. Following Master Deim's broad back, Johanna grabbed the branches as she went, and they showed her Loesie running over this path, wildly crashing into willow trunks. Her eyes were wide, but still had their normal colour. She ran bent over, as if she'd hurt herself.

Master Deim shouted, "By the heavens."

He stopped and Johanna peered around him.

Loesie sat cross-legged in the middle of a patch of grass, her back straight. In one hand, she held a blood-stained knife, and she was using the sharp point to score her skin. She had already made a network of bleeding cuts on her left arm.

She had discarded all her clothes, and was meticulously cutting the skin of her upper left leg, her face unemotional.

Tracks of blood trailed over her pale skin and dripped onto the ground.

She was so absorbed in her task that she didn't notice Master Deim or Johanna, but just kept cutting, her face scrunched in concentration.

Then she looked up, turning to Loesie and Master Deim. She had also scored her cheeks. Blood dripped down her jaw onto her chest.

She slowly wiped her hands over her stomach, smearing blood on the pale skin. She *massaged* her stomach, arching her back, all the while moaning.

"By the heavens," Master Deim said again.

Loesie laughed.

No, the demon had not gone at all. The demon might have been asleep for a while, but it had been with her all that time. It had probably been awakened when Loesie tried to drive off the magical apparition on the riverbank.

"Come," Johanna said, holding out a hand.

Loesie just stared, resting her hand on her stomach. Trails of blood had run between her fingers over the back of her hand.

"Put down the knife," Johanna said.

Loesie looked at the hand that held the knife, the point still poking at the skin. A flicker of disturbance went over her face as if she saw her bleeding arms for the first time.

She dropped the knife in the grass. Her face went pale.

Master Deim rushed in behind her and picked it up.

Loesie dragged her dress over her naked body, her eyes wide, her mouth open. Her hands trembled and the skin had gone purple. She smeared blood everywhere.

"I think I'm going to be sick," she said weakly, and illustrated it by vomiting all over one side of the dress. It was mostly slime and blood, but made even more of a mess of the garment.

"Oh, look at it now," she cried and she vomited again. In her effort to miss the dress, it went all over Johanna's hands, mostly brown foamy slime.

"I'm sorry, I'm sorry." She let the soaked dress drop to her knees.

"I don't mind," Johanna said, looking at Loesie's bloodied skin.

"Come, let's go home." She picked up Loesie's discarded dress and held it up. Apart from the fact that it was wet, the bottom part had been slashed into ribbons. But it would have to do.

"Try to put this on. We're going back to the *Lady Sara*."

Although she wasn't sure if she wanted Loesie sleeping in the same cabin as Nellie with knives in the galley next door.

The wildness had gone from Loesie's eyes and Johanna managed to get Loesie back into the dress. Her cloak, muddy as it was, covered most of the gaping rips in her dress where the skin shone through. In a shallow part of the bank, she made Loesie wash herself, shivering and in stiff and jerky movements.

Very carefully, with Master Deim helping her, they guided Loesie along the path. While she complained of being cold, her skin felt hot and dry. When they came close to the camp, Master Deim ran ahead to get a blanket, but still they got plenty of stares.

Nellie stood on the deck of the *Lady Sara*. She watched with wide eyes and covered her mouth with her hands while Johanna and Master Deim shuffled up the gangplank with Loesie between them.

She retreated once they were on the deck, her face pale.

In the cabin, Johanna cleaned Loesie's cuts. Most of them were shallow and would heal by themselves. She put ointment and bandages over some of the deeper ones. Nellie stood by the doorway, her face still pale. No one said anything.

The uneasy silence lingered until Nellie asked how Loesie got all those cuts and in response to being told exclaimed, "She did it herself? Who cuts their own skin?"

Loesie snorted and Johanna intervened before it could come to an outburst. "Maybe you would like to bring Loesie some tea."

"Yes, mistress Johanna, immediately."

Johanna sat on the edge of the bed watching Nellie's back as she ran from the cabin. *Nellie, one day your trusting nature is going to hurt you badly.*

A bit of colour had returned to Loesie's cheeks.

"Is there anything we should know about?"

Loesie shook her head.

"You're sure about that? Then why *did* you do this?"

Loesie shook her head again.

Johanna's heart jumped. This was so much like when she had first met Loesie at the markets, when she had lost her voice. "Can you still speak?"

"Yes, just not about that. Not his name. I don't know his name, all right?" Her eyes went wide again.

"Calm down, calm down." This was the closest Loesie had come to admitting that someone had bewitched her. She must not lose Loesie's trust. "When did this happen?"

"In early spring, before the trees started sprouting leaves."

"At the farm?"

She nodded. Her lip trembled. "Annette is dead because of me. Ma is dead because of me. Granpa and Granma are dead because of me!" He voice rose.

"Shhh." Johanna held Loesie's shoulders. She felt hot and dry. *Like a demon's fire.*

"Please, if you care for me, leave me alone," Loesie whispered. "Give me the knife and let me kill myself."

"Don't be silly. We'll find someone to help you."

Nellie came with tea and after having made sure that Loesie drank some, Johanna left to go to the hold. She felt so tired. Being here, in this place infused with magic, tired everyone out. They would have to move soon, or risk staying here forever.

In the hold, Roald sat at the desk by the light of a flickering oil lamp, intently staring at a piece of paper. In typical fashion, he didn't look up when she came in.

"What are you doing?"

"That's the symbol of the Burovian royal family."

"What is?"

He showed her the sheet of paper. It was her crude drawing of the key on the back of Shepherd Carolus' abductor's hood.

Johanna's heart thudded. "Is there anyone from the Burovian royal family at the work farm?"

"Prince Hugo," Roald said, pulling a face. "I don't like him at all. He whips the horses and kicks the piglets."

"Does he have dark hair that he wears in a ponytail?"

He frowned at her. "I think so."

"Is he still at the farm?"

"Yes, he is one of the bosses."

Johanna couldn't believe that the answer they had been looking for had been here all the time.

The Baroness had lied about the symbol. She would have recognised it and known who it belonged to. Likely, the nobles knew it, too. So they had taken the Shepherd to the farm? If they were magicians then what did they want with him? A chill went over her back.

"Could you . . . help me get there?"

CHAPTER 17

JOHANNA GOT UP very early the next morning, and went into the misty pre-dawn to ask Master Deim for the loan of a boat, which he said he'd bring along later.

She rushed back to the camp and in the cabin of the *Lady Sara*, she got herself and Roald dressed *for another adventure*. Roald asked if they were going to listen to wood again, and Johanna said they might, but nerves knotted in her gut. She could eat only little of the porridge brought by Nellie. Loesie was still asleep, Nellie said, and it was probably better to leave her like that.

The problem of Loesie was one Johanna would have to solve later.

Out on the deck, the mist still hadn't lifted, muffling sounds and keeping animals silent.

Two people were walking up the jetty towards the *Lady Sara*. When they came up the gangplank Johanna recognised the first one as Master Deim, and the second one turned out to be a young man.

"This is Karl," Master Deim said.

The young man nodded a greeting. He had a severe face

that looked too old for his age, all planes and angles. He wore local dress.

"Karl is a cousin of mine by marriage. His family is not in the pay of the duke or the Guentherite order, and his uncle is the Holy Father Lucius of the main church. If anything goes wrong or the Guentherites make threats to you, they won't want to give his uncle a reason to complain. The Guentherites are not on good footing with people in the town, but they rely on us for many of their supplies. Karl will be your shield."

"Thank you."

"Karl has also visited the Guentherites and worked for them, so he is well-versed in their ways."

The young man didn't look old enough to have had those experiences. "Thank you," Johanna said again. "You are really a most useful friend. I do hope that when we return to oust Alexandre, you will come with us."

Master Deim smiled, but said nothing. What did that mean? Was he coming? Was he staying here? There was no time to talk about it.

Last night, Johanna had tied up two sea cows in preparation for this expedition and now she reeled in the ropes of both. The animals were strong males, placid if a bit lazy, but they came to the bank for the cabbage leaves she held in the water. Their big snouts with the rough whiskers brushed her hand. She tied both in the small harness which had hung at the back of the cabin for all of the journey, and tied the ropes to the small rowing boat that Master Deim had brought.

On a whim, she threw the rest of the cabbage in the water and reeled in the ropes of all the animals. She met Master Deim's eyes while doing so. He nodded in silent understanding. *Just in case we'll need to get out of here quickly.*

Roald climbed into the little boat, taking the reins from

her. With a bit of training, he would probably be much better at handling sea cows than she would ever be.

Karl seemed a little uncertain about the animals and sat on the bench as far as possible from them.

They set off.

At first, no one spoke. Water slapped against the sides of the boat. Johanna didn't dare look too deeply into its murkiness. She didn't need to study the water to see the ghostly forms swirling underneath. Occasionally one of the animals would break the surface with a flipper or snout, or would come up to take in a deep and noisy breath. She had to steer the boat upstream first so that they could drift back to the jetty on the other side with the current.

From here, it was clear that the Guentherite farm lay on a slight hill and that its buildings and belltower overlooked the surrounding land.

The boat came past the run-off of a creek where a lot of cloudy water joined the river. The creek ran between a couple of paddocks into the Guentherite order's land. Thin veils of mist hung over those paddocks and the banks of the creek.

Upriver from that branch, the colour of the water became darker and clearer.

"A branch of the river splits off and goes around the back of that hill," Roald said. "The abbot got the workers to dig a new creek so that they could build a water mill there."

"So the cloudiness is run-off from mud?" Johanna asked. From where they were, upstream of the creek, the change in colour was very clear.

"Is that mill working now?" Karl asked. It was the first thing he said in their presence, although he still seemed a little uncertain about how to relate to Roald. "Last time I saw it, they were still building it. They had some strange problems with it, I understand."

"The mill is working," Roald said.

The boat turned back downstream, and then drifted back to the jetty.

Johanna caught the post, and Roald threw the rope over and pulled the boat in. A rickety wooden ladder showed that the monks were prepared for times of low water, but those stairs were not needed today.

Johanna loosened the harness and the two bulls wandered off to graze.

A gravel-paved path ran from the jetty to the low buildings of the order set on the hill. The belltower of the chapel that Roald had talked about overlooked the fields.

The place looked completely peaceful, with rows of grapes with yellowing leaves and cows grazing in the paddock. A faint mist hung over the fields. From here, Florisheim looked pretty with the Baron's castle and its fat, stubby tower protruding from the jumble of slate-covered roofs. From here, the quay looked barren and menacing, with the city wall and its iron gates at the back. While the city gate that Johanna passed on the way into town from the camp had always been open, these gates facing the river were always closed. Two ships lay there, low river freight vessels like the *Lady Sara*, but less pretty.

The gated entrances to the cellars underneath the quay were also closed, and most of them were too far under water for any type of boat to enter.

Behind her, Roald said, "Uh-oh."

Johanna's heart jumped and she looked back at their side of the river, expecting to see someone coming down the path. But there was no one. Cows grazed. A group of geese came waddling down the hill.

"What's the matter?"

"Don't like geese," he said, nervously looking over his shoulder. "You know that I once got bitten by a goose?"

Johanna laughed. "You're afraid of geese?"

"You'd be afraid, too, if you knew these geese. They are not nice."

Meanwhile, the geese waddled, honking down the path.

"Let's go this way." Roald pulled her sleeve.

He led them onto a side path between two fields of grapes. The path was narrow and muddy, and they had to walk single-file. The grapes grew in rows on trellises that reached above their heads, so that they couldn't see what happened elsewhere. Johanna thought of the tunnel of interwoven trees on Duke Lothar's land. The vines were heavy with fat, dew-covered red grapes. Roald picked a small bunch and shared them around. "The skins are touch, but just spit them out."

The grapes looked sweet, but they tasted sour. The skins were indeed quite inedible. Roald ate and spat, but she felt like she had to be more civilised about it, and wormed the skins into her hand before dropping them onto the ground.

"Who would want fruit as sour as this?"

"They're for making wine," Roald said, and went on to explain how wine was made. Apparently, it involved men stomping through grapes with their bare feet.

Then they came over the crest of the hill where the vineyards stopped.

Here there were orchards full of apples, that would soon need to be harvested, and stands of berries bleeding into pine forest.

Johanna couldn't help but think that some of these fruits should have been harvested in the past few days when the weather had been warm.

A couple of horses grazed in a paddock.

Roald whistled.

One of the animals, a brown stallion, pricked up his ears, and turned his head in Roald's direction.

Roald ran to the fence and slapped his hand on the top bar. "Come here, Selmus! Come here, come here."

Silly. Of course his friends on the farm had been animals. Johanna should have known that.

The horse clopped to the fence. Roald climbed on top so he could better reach the horse's face. It nuzzled his face, whickering. Roald petted its head and scratched between the ears. If he could rule the animal kingdom, Roald would be the best king ever.

"Shouldn't we go?" Johanna looked over her shoulders, nervous that someone would come. The plan was to try to find Shepherd Carolus, without being discovered, and smuggle him out.

"They feed the animals in the mornings," Roald said. "No one comes here for most of the day while they're all working."

"Aren't they working in the fields?" Although by the neglected look of the vineyards, she should have known the answer. And neglecting the harvest seemed the most stupid thing to do ever. If the religious order sold wine and dried fruit, then what would they eat for the rest of the year if they didn't get those grapes in?

"You'll see."

Roald jumped down from the fence. They continued down the hill. The horse followed them as far as it could. Most of the mist had cleared, but veils of it still hung in the valley, covering a little thicket of oak trees, where a small tower protruded from the canopy of leaves. Water pooled in a small lake in front of the trees. The surface was smooth as glass and reflected the trees and the chapel on the far bank. It was all so peaceful that Johanna couldn't imagine that people who lived here did any ill.

But when they came close to the chapel, it was as if the

mist increased and the day grew darker. There were also . . . strange noises. Hammering, the grinding of millstones.

"Is there a water mill here?"

"I told you they diverted a part of the river to go through the fields so that they could have a mill here."

Yes, he had told her. It just seemed an unlikely place for a water mill, right next to the chapel, supposedly a place of prayer and solitude.

On the other side of the chapel, trees had been cleared from an area that covered both banks of the creek. The water fell down a man-made drop, operating the watermill at good speed. The silence of the forest was broken by the steady slosh-slosh of the water in the scoops and the creaking and clanking of the mechanism. Whatever the mill operated was under the ground, connected by a large beam and two gear wheels and a second beam which went into a hole at least twenty paces across. Johanna couldn't see over the edge, but sounds of clanking and rattling mill wheels rose from below.

"Do they make paper here?" It was a strange place for that, with not even a roof overhead.

"No. This is where they make iron."

Iron? Wasn't that something people got . . . from the mountains?

Johanna crept closer, but even when she could see the mechanisms and moving mill wheels in that hole in the ground, she still couldn't see the bottom of the pit. The beam went deep into the ground, still turning, to whatever mechanism it operated down there. It squeaked.

The pit appeared to be man-dug, with walls fortified with trunks of pine saplings. A ramp made from crude planks of wood zigzagged down into the pit. The air was moist here, and misty. It smelled of wet earth and reminded her in a disturbing, unpleasant way of the ice cellar.

She could almost smell the faint rank scent of beginning decay.

A monk in a grey habit came up a ramp wheeling a barrow full of what looked like black gravel. He went a short distance into the shelter of a roof on the other side of the pit and upended his load on top of a heap of similar material. Someone else was shovelling rocks from another pile into another machine that looked like grinding stones.

There was a huge brick furnace at the back of the shed. Another set of beams and wheels went in that direction, coming from a second water mill, and moved a giant bellows up and down that fanned the flames in the furnace. The entrance of the furnace was open and a monk was shovelling in scoops full of the black dirt.

On the far end of the furnace, another monk lifted out a long pole with, on the end, a stone bowl with red glowing fluid inside. Another came to help and they poured it into a stone mould.

Wait—she recognised these two. They weren't proper monks. They were the two men she had sent downriver as scouts. She raised a hand to her mouth to stop herself shouting out. All that time the people in the camp had been waiting for them to return.

Both men looked dirty. The hollow expressions on their faces spoke of days of hard work and little chance of escape.

On the floor lay finished blocks of metal, sheets and strange shapes. Some monks were fashioning glowing shapes with hammers before they cooled down too much.

In this open shed, Johanna recognised Shepherd Carolus, dressed in one of the grey gowns, stacking blocks of iron on top of each other. His arms had several raw wounds and bruises. His face was sweaty with the work.

"There are three of our people here," she said in a low voice to Karl, who had not met the Shepherd. She wasn't afraid of being heard. The noise of the mill and the rushing water would down out their voices.

"Are there people guarding this place?" Karl asked.

"It's easy to escape work," Roald said. "Not so easy to stay away from punishment. The forests on all sides are full of dangerous things, and the monks will hunt you down and punish you."

Karl nodded.

Shepherd Carolus now stood with his back to them, lifting another heavy piece on top of the pile.

"What in heaven's name do they need that much iron for?" Johanna asked. She knew about swords and various farming tools, but couldn't think why anyone needed huge piece of iron, flat sheets, curved sheets, and chunky pieces with holes, presumably for handles, but the pieces looked like no tool she had ever seen.

"It's for making machines," Roald said.

"What kind?" He'd talked about these *machines* for a bit, and like many things Roald said, she had not taken him seriously. Did that mean that birds could indeed fly to the Moon?

"The black rock is what makes the fire burn so hot. They find it in the ground in that hole over there. It's extremely deep. There are tunnels down there and it's very wet and dirty. When people come out they're black all over. The iron rocks they get from a little way up the river where they've made another hole. They put those rocks on a barge and let it float down the river. Then they crush it and heat it up in the furnace and they can pour the iron."

A couple of monks were now lifting a platform full of hexagonal shapes that still glowed with heat. One of the monks only had one hand, which he used to lower the platform in the water with rope and pulleys. The water boiled and hissed, releasing a cloud of steam that hid the monks from view.

Johanna pulled Roald back and Karl followed a little bit into the forest.

"How are we going to get them out?" She looked from Roald to Karl and back again. "Maybe at night? Can you show us where they sleep?"

Roald shook his head. "There are geese near the main buildings."

"Do we have to worry about geese?" Karl asked. "They're only birds."

"They make a lot of noise," Johanna said. Besides, if Roald didn't want to do something, it was best not to do it.

Karl gave her an incredulous look in an *and-you-believe-that-we-should-be-afraid-of-geese?* way.

"What is the path they normally use to go back to the buildings?" Johanna asked. "The same one we've used?"

"No, there is another path. I'll show you."

The area behind the chapel was covered in thick forest. Roald led the group over various animal tracks that led through the tangle.

The sound of the thumping mill wheels and falling water faded before becoming stronger again.

They arrived at the top of another waterfall, this one not yet with a mill, although a hollowed-out area in the opposite bank showed that one was planned there. The water that tumbled over the edge into a deep pond was murky, as if someone had spilled milk in the creek upstream. A fine mist spread at the spot where the waterfall hit the pond's surface, and swirls of fine silt formed cloudy shapes under the surface. This was where the river downstream obtained its muddy colour.

It was as if the clouds consisted of tiny particles of silver that, when they swirled, reflected the light like schools of tiny fish. Johanna crouched and reached for the water, wanting to stir it up.

"Don't touch," Karl said. "The water is bad. Don't touch it and don't drink it."

All right. She straightened.

But then, a thought: what about the camp? It was downstream and people had been drinking this water for months.

They had also behaved too passively for months. She had wondered what made them like this and now she knew why.

"Magic," Johanna said, softly. She stared at the pond, watching the swirling shapes under the surface. At times she swore she could see people or faces.

Roald said, "When I was here, Alexandre fell in and the ghosts nearly killed him. That was why they said he went mad."

Johanna couldn't stop looking at the water. It called out to her, making the magic in her blood sing.

Someone has disturbed the magic lines. The meaning of that warning was now clear.

The digging in the ground by the monks had done this. Magic bled out of the ground with the water that the monks used to cool their iron and rinse their rocks.

"So, if we're not going to get them from the dorm, then what do we do?" Karl said. He stood a bit back from the water, clamping his hands around himself, staring out over the mist. The bell tower of the main chapel protruded from above the buildings on top of the hill.

"We wait until the workers start going home, and then we'll try to get the Shepherd's attention. He's a strong man and I'm sure he can run. I presume they follow that path over there to the house."

Roald nodded. "Yes, they go that way, and then up the hill and between the vineyards to the back of the main building. There is a chicken pen there, and they have ducks. The geese don't live near that part of the building. I think they don't like the ducks. Oh, and there is also a donkey, but it's not very friendly. You have to be careful, because it kicks."

"What time do they go back to the building?"

"Usually when it goes dark."

That meant a long wait. It also meant that even after they freed the men, they might have to stay out here overnight because it might be too dark to cross the river.

The thought of staying here overnight gave her the chills.

CHAPTER 18

THERE WAS NO COVER closer to the house, so they had to wait in the forest. Roald stretched out on the grass and was soon asleep, but Johanna felt uneasy. She spent a good while studying the shapes in the water. If she squinted, she could see them bleeding into the pool over the edge of the waterfall and re-forming once they were in the pond. She walked a little way back where she could see the cloudy water run out of the pit that the monks used to cool the iron. A stream of particularly milky water flowed out of a clay pipe that came from the deeper hole.

At regular intervals, a monk would come up the ramp out of that hole with a wheelbarrow full of black stuff. As Roald had said, his face was black as soot, and this made his eyes look oddly bright. He would wheel his load to the furnace, tip it over and go back down.

The water mill creaked, the huge bellows made a "whoomp" noise every time the air was pressed out into the furnace. Sometimes, fire would blow out of little air holes on the side.

Shepherd Carolus was still stacking the iron shapes. A

cart had arrived with two huge horses and he was loading the iron pieces onto the tray. Whenever he stopped for a rest, one of the overseers would yell. This was the only time that the horses would twitch or turn their heads. They were *very* huge, with long fetlocks and big, fat rumps. She wondered if Roald knew these horses, too.

She counted at least fifteen men in the clearing and under the shelter, but there might be more in the hole where she couldn't see them. Some of those men would be supervisors, like the one with the embroidered key on his robe, the Burovian prince, but others looked like workers or, more correctly, prisoners.

The sun came through, its light weak through the mist, and then sank towards the horizon.

They sat between the trees and ate. The bread they had brought was dry and hard to swallow.

Karl looked really nervous, and when Johanna asked him why he was so jumpy, he only said that, "Strange things happen here at night." He wouldn't elaborate on what those things were, at which Roald started reciting a dissertation about *ghosts and other things unnatural*, written, he assured Johanna and Karl, by a priest of the Belaman Church. Strangely enough, it did nothing help Karl's nerves.

As dusk slid over the land, a few lights came on in the windows of the main building, but the whoomping of the bellows kept going and no one in the hole or in the shed with the furnace was preparing to stop work. Did these people go to sleep at all?

The Moon rose over the horizon like a giant orange orb and spread an eerie pale glow over the fields. In it, and the rising mist, shapes swirled over the surface of the water.

The thumping and creaking in the forest clearing continued unabated. A second cart approached over the main road from the main farm buildings.

"They're using Selmus," Roald whispered next to Johanna while they watched the two horses pull the cart at leisurely pace towards the forest. The cart did not come back, nor did the one that was already there.

"Do you know where they take those iron shapes?" Johanna asked.

Roald said, "A place down the river that's called Willow Bend. It's the abbot's summer residence. It's quite close to Aroden."

"And what do they do with them there?"

"Make machines."

"But whatever for?" Also, she had come up that river, but had not seen the abbot's summer residence, unless it had been around the bend from where the bandits had captured them.

Maybe . . . her thoughts whirled.

Maybe the abbot hadn't *wanted* anyone to see whatever happened at his summer residence and maybe that was the real reason they had been captured.

If that was the case, then it made sense that the men who had travelled down the river had never reached Saardam.

But there was no time to contemplate it further, because something was happening at the main building now.

A door had opened in the wall that faced the forest and a group of men came out, walking in a long line over the path. There were at least twenty of them, all dressed in robes. The first few in the group carried something between them that looked suspiciously like a body on a stretcher. Several of the men in the tail of the procession held candles, and the glow from the flames was reminiscent of fireflies: little pinpricks of light that did little to dispel the darkness.

When they had reached the end of the path between the vineyards, the stretcher-bearers turned towards the pond.

Lying on her belly on the ground, Johanna shuffled backwards so that they wouldn't see her. She sensed Roald and Karl behind her.

The line came closer and stopped at the edge of the pool, where the group gathered around their leader. He spoke, but his words were drowned out by the water rushing over the ledge and falling into the pond below. The mist that rose from the pond was rendered almost luminous by the moonlight.

They group shuffled aside to let the men with the stretcher to the water's edge. The thing under the cloth was definitely a body. The shape of the toes and the head pushed up the fabric.

Two other men dropped two planks of wood across two rows of stones that protruded from the water. The stretcher-bearers walked across these and lowered the stretcher into the water. One of the men pulled the cloth away.

The dead man's pale gown glowed in the moonlight. His skin was waxy pale and bore darker scars and spots as if he'd died of pox. Johanna shivered. Father had told her of the ravages of the pox epidemics in Estland and Gelre. For some reason, the disease had never done much in Saardam, but that could easily change.

The monks on both sides pulled the stretcher out from under him.

The body floated.

A man stepped forward from the group of spectators. Whereas most of the monks wore grey robes, his cloak was very dark brown or black, but unadorned, so he was not the Burovian prince, who, she thought, was still at the shed in the forest.

While the others watched, he raised his hands and started some sort of incantation. From her position at the top of the waterfall, Johanna couldn't make out any of the words.

For a while, Johanna thought this was a ritual for a monk

who had died. She thought that once they had cleansed the body, the men would cover it up, carry it away and bury it elsewhere.

And damn it, now she noticed how the clanking of the water wheel and the whoomping of the bellows behind her had stopped, and the voices of men rang through the forest. The work party was about to stop for the night. They would walk over the road to the main building and now it would be difficult to attract the attention of Shepherd Carolus and the two others, let alone allow them to escape, with all these people here.

"Look!" Karl whispered.

Because something happened in the pond as well.

Tendrils of mist rose from the water and enveloped the body until it was encased in a misty gown. Slowly, the body sank under the surface with sucking and wet crunching sounds as if some sea creature was chewing it up. But the water was perfectly still.

The dark-robed man continued to stand at the bank with his hands raised towards the heavens. The monks watched, silent sentinels to this macabre spectacle.

Johanna was feeling ill to the stomach.

The mist released the body which bobbed back up. After hearing those sounds, Johanna was half-surprised to see it intact.

The body kept rising and rising until it came free of the water and floated in the air. The black-robed man held his hands higher, as if pulling it up by invisible strings. His voice rose into a crescendo, but although the words were clear, the meaning of them was not. Johanna didn't even know what language he spoke.

The body *twitched*. Eyes opened. Hands jerked. The man sat up, looking out of hollow, empty eyes. His mouth opened and he sighed out a hissing breath, but no other sound came out.

Karl, on the ground next to her, let out a muffled squeak.

"Be quiet!" Johanna whispered.

The apparition floated away from the bank and until it hovered over the middle of the pond. Like Princess Celine, it didn't look ethereal enough to be a ghost, and the colours of the skin and hair were too washed-out for a real person.

The black-robed man asked a question. The apparition turned away from him.

The man asked the question again.

The apparition now floated to the other side of the pond, closest to Johanna, Karl and Roald. Its skin shone with pale luminous light.

Judging by his finely-made nightgown, the man had been someone of higher standing in real life. Someone who would have died suddenly of a hidden illness and whose family would have the means to allow magicians to experiment with trying to return him to life?

But this man wasn't alive, and he wasn't a ghost with unfinished business to take care of, like the ghosts of people who had been murdered or died violently.

The man in the dark robe was now yelling at him from the far edge of the pond, the volume and tone of his voice rising, but the apparition did acknowledge him in any way.

The robed man gave a roar of frustration, balling his fists at the sky. He kicked the water, grabbed a stick and whirled around. All the surrounding monks backed away. He whirled at the pond, lifting the stick above his head and slammed it into the water. A great spray of drops flew up, glittering in the moonlight.

The apparition turned around in an annoyed way. It hissed, the sound so soft that it was barely perceptible, but it made Johanna's hair stand up. A cold breeze tracked over the water, disturbing the mist. The black-robed man said something, the tone mocking. Johanna caught something about the meaning of magic. The other monks retreated even further. The robed man laughed at them. There was something eerily familiar about that laugh, but Johanna couldn't see into the shadow of his hood.

The ghostly apparition floated towards him. The robed man grabbed waved his stick in front of him. He was still laughing. The apparition lashed at him, but the stick sliced through the ghost and cut off one of its ethereal arms. It hung uselessly in the air. The ghost stared at it, as if surprised. The black-robed man took the moment of surprise to cut the ghost in half at the waist, distributing swirls of mist over the surface of the water.

The two halves of the apparition drifted down and bled into misty shapes that sank into the surface of the pond. They were absorbed by the water until there was nothing left.

Next to Johanna, Karl let out a relieved sigh.

But then the water started to churn and boil. Something long and thin broke the surface: an insect's leg the thickness of a human arm, with bristles over its surface. And then another leg and another. The creature that rose from the water was not the same as the one as she had seen earlier. It was bigger and had more legs, and as its long body emerged from the water, more and more legs appeared, like a giant centipede. It reared and reared, until its head faced Johanna.

Karl screamed and ran.

Roald hid behind a tree, leaving Johanna standing by herself on top of the waterfall. There was nowhere to go and she had nothing to defend herself. She scrambled on the forest floor for a stick of wood, but there was none.

Slowly, she retreated, step by step, never losing the creature from sight. It swayed and wriggled its legs. It would be deadly if it chose to attack.

The black-robed man yelled, his hands outstretched. The creature twisted its long and glistening body around, and hissed at the man, who didn't move. He kept his hands outstretched, and kept chanting his strange words. His voice echoed over the water, a strong sonorous sound.

The creature froze. The luminous mist that made up its body lost its glow. The trees on the other side of the pond showed through its ethereal form. Slowly, its legs became thinner and grew shorter. Its body dissolved in swirls of mist which thinned and merged with the regular mist that hung over the water, until it had disappeared completely.

Johanna stared at the moonlit mist where the creature had been. There was not a breath of wind, no sound except for the distant call of a bird. The group of monks still stood on the other side of the pond, staring at her.

Slowly, the black-robed man lowered his hood. His face was surprisingly young, freckled, and his chin had the hint of a beard. He wore his red curly hair tied at the nape of his neck. She knew that face, and had seen that hair before.

It was Kylian.

CHAPTER 19

THERE WAS NO further point in hiding. Kylian had seen Johanna, although he might not have seen Roald and Karl.

She took her time to pick her way down the incline to the edge of the pond. While she did this, she stole glances at the group of monks who had come with him. Most of them looked disturbed and were still staring at the water. Oh no, she didn't think that the apparition had been killed. Neither had the one that looked like Princess Celine been destroyed when Loesie fought it. They were just waiting under the surface to strike again at Kylian's command.

Kylian looked straight at her. "Finally we meet again, little princess. I've been looking forward to this."

"What are you doing here?" Her heart thudded. No, she didn't want him anywhere near her. He was dangerous.

He bowed his head in a mockery of courtesy. "I was waiting to see your pretty face."

Johanna's mouth seemed to have frozen up. All she could think of was how, when she'd attended the ball, he'd swept her up in a dance in the gallery behind the ballroom in the palace and how he'd kissed her.

Johanna wanted to scream that she didn't want him near her, that he was an evil magician.

She wanted to tell the monks about the bodies in the ice cellar, that Kylian was a necromancer, but they probably knew all this already, and saying it out loud would make him angry and more dangerous.

She wanted to run, but she didn't think that her legs would support her. It was her own fault this had happened. She should never have come here.

But now that she had come down to the water, she recognised the Shepherd Carolus as one of the onlookers behind the monks. His eyes were wide and mouth hung open. When their eyes met, his lips moved. "Johanna?"

Johanna resisted the urge to check over her shoulder to see if Roald and Karl were still hidden, but that would give her companions away, although Kylian might already know about them.

Kylian walked slowly around the pond until he faced her.

Johanna wanted to back away, to run from him as far as she could, but she kept her ground, her back straight. If anything, her stubbornness would give Roald enough time to flee, if he was smart enough.

Kylian was now very close. In the moonlight, his hair looked brown. He reached out a hand to her cheek.

Johanna stepped back. She didn't want the hands that had touched a dead body to touch her. She didn't want to give Roald a reason to come storming down that hill to yell for Kylian to *keep your hands off my women.*

He chuckled. "You don't trust me."

"That's an understatement. Why should I trust you? After this evil magic I just saw you perform?"

"I saved much of your beloved city." He put his hand

inside his cloak, withdrew a large splinter of wood and held it out to her.

Johanna covered her hand with her cloak before taking it from him.

He chuckled. "I see you've learned."

"What's this?" She held up the splinter meeting his eyes over its pointy end.

"Touch it. You will see." His expression was intense.

She lowered her hand. "I don't think I will. I've already seen far too many things I never wished I had, starting with that night in Saardam. I have no desire to see more blood or more fire or more dead bodies."

She held the splinter out in the space between them and dropped it. It fell, point first, into the mud.

Did he flinch or was that her imagination?

"You don't want to know what I did to save much of your city?"

"No, because I don't believe you. You came to Saardam to take possession of it. You took Alexandre Trebuchet and then washed your hands of him. But in truth, though you and your family may not like him, he's your minion more than anyone else's."

"You should learn the facts before you accuse people. Did we not see the fire demons from the back of the palace? Did I not run from the garden to help fight them? I knew none of the locals had any aptitude with magic, so I went to fight it. Magic is drawn by magic, as you will well understand."

"I have no idea what you did."

"Then pick up that piece of wood, and it will show you."

Johanna glanced down, but couldn't see it in the grass. She hesitated. Should she look for it? But no, she didn't trust him. And wood showed things that happened in the place where it was part of a table or a door. It showed snatches of conversation, people walking past. It rarely added up to a coherent story, unless he'd carried this piece with him for the *purpose* of telling the story, in which case she definitely didn't trust him. "Anyway, why would you fight it? You weren't in your town."

"We were in Saardam as guests of the king. Royal families help each other, as you will probably still need to learn."

Was that an underhand jab?

Why was he even at the ball? The ties between the Baron, the royal family and this monastery that was a place for unruly royal sons were far from clear.

"What were you doing in the middle of the night at Duke Lothar's castle? What were you doing, trying to interrogate my maid, but clearing out before you could speak to me? If you were so helpful, you might have introduced yourself to the new king of Saarland."

"I was there on other business, visiting a mentor in an outlying town. I often go to the Duke's castle to stay overnight when I'm travelling. He's my uncle."

"He tried to murder your father."

He laughed. "Oh, you've heard that story."

"What's so funny about it?"

"It was a practical joke. My uncle and my father are not enemies at all."

That was not how she understood it.

"My uncle helps my father quite a bit. Seeing as you like to talk about how we all have court magicians, my uncle could be called my father's court magician."

And who had told him that she'd been talking about court magicians?

"I don't believe that at all. The Duke and his son were very clear about where they stand. Where is your father anyway and why won't he talk to any of us? Why do you keep people here against their will? What are you doing here in the middle of the night with dead bodies?" She had to stop to draw breath. There were so many more questions she could have asked.

But it didn't matter, because he wasn't going to reply anyway. He was just going to dance around the issue and play with her as a cat plays with a mouse. That mouse again. She glanced at Shepherd Carolus.

"I'm here to say that you won't need to put up with me much longer. We'll leave as soon as possible, something we should have done long ago. Whatever is going on in Saardam, and you're not telling us, is not going to be fought from here."

She turned away from him but took only one step before he grabbed her upper arm in a strong grip.

"Not so fast, princess, where do you think you're going?" He was close enough that she could see the moonlight glisten in his eyelashes. The light fell sideways into his eyes and brought out all the intricate bumps, flecks and veins in his irises.

"I'm going back to the *Lady Sara*. We're going home."

"You think you can handle fire magic now? Do you have that magician you were looking for so desperately?"

Seriously, had Magda told everyone in town? "No, but is battling him without magic any worse than sitting here until we die and then being consumed by ghosts? This land is rife with magic. None of our people can handle it, and it's like we're slowly being poisoned."

"How about I help you?"

"You?" She met his eyes and for a moment, wanted to say yes. Because he might not yet be fully versed in necromancy, but she knew no one near as powerful.

But what was his relationship with Alexandre?

"You're still distrusting? I told you then that I could help you and I'm telling you now."

"A lot has changed."

"Nothing has changed in the world of magic at all. Magic

is attracted by magic. You can feel magic in me. You are attracted to me."

"You have far too high an opinion of yourself."

"Why did you marry the Idiot Prince? Why, when you should have come with me and received training in magic?"

"And then what? What are you anyway? How do I know that you don't have anything to do with Alexandre Trebuchet? How do I know that you didn't send him? How do I know what the lot of you want from us? I do not believe that Alexandre acted by himself of his own accord, and I don't believe that you don't know what is going on. Now let me go and keep your hands off me."

"All right, all right." He stepped back, holding up his hands.

Johanna rubbed her upper arm.

"Then don't believe me. I can't make you. After all, someone who believes in that hideous three-headed monster has clearly lost his mind. Go on being a happy little queen without an heir."

Something snapped inside her. She lashed out and hit Kylian in the face with a slap that echoed over the water. Several of the monks gasped.

Shepherd Carolus looked at her with wide eyes.

Kylian grabbed her wrist and pulled her close. "That's more like it." He was so close that she could feel the warmth of his breath. It smelled nutty with a faint trace of liquor. "Keep up the anger. You can't fight without anger. One day I might even tell you why you don't yet have an heir."

His face hovered over hers. For a moment, she thought he was going to kiss her again, and there was nothing she could do to stop him. Already her magic was singing out to him and part of her wanted it. She was hoping the Roald would come down to the water and go into one of his rages about *his women* but he did not. Again, Roald was smarter than she thought. Or maybe he had been captured already.

She pulled her arm. "Can you let me go? I've come here to speak to the abbot about our Shepherd and the other two men you hold prisoner. I don't know why they are here, but I'd like to take them with me."

"You—what?" Kylian started laughing. Shepherd Carolus was shaking his head, his eyes wide. "You have the hide to come in here and ask—what?"

Johanna tried to gesture with her eyes. *Run, run!*

"Why were they taken? What are you doing with them? What are you doing in that hole in the ground?"

"You would like to know all that?" His fingertips dug into the soft flesh of her upper arm. He chuckled. "You would really like to know all that, eh?"

Johanna met his hard gaze, trying hard to maintain her uncompromising stance. But his magic ate at her. *Just give in,* it said. *There is no way you can fight him,* it said.

"I can tell you, but then I'd have to kill you." He trailed the finger of his free hand over her nose, leaving behind a trail of tingling where his skin had touched hers. Part of her wanted to say *Kill me tomorrow morning, and it will all have been worth it*. She shook her head to force those silly thoughts from her mind. He was evil, a dark magician of the worst kind.

He paused his finger at her chin. "Or I could tell you, and I'd have to kill that idiot of a husband of yours."

No, Roald. He knew Roald was here. Maybe his men had captured Roald already.

"Or I could take you up to the dining hall, order a nice dinner of food grown on the farm and tell you over a good glass of wine. I get quite lonely. I'll let your hapless companions go in return, and I'll even tell you a secret or two that will help you to get rid of that useless oaf Alexandre."

Johanna met his brown eyes. She had to do whatever she could to distract him men so that Roald and Karl could escape. "You're kidding, right?"

"No, I'm not. The choice is not so difficult, is it?"

"Just dinner?"

"Just dinner."

Johanna took a deep breath. She didn't believe him for one moment. He was going to take advantage of her, show her horrible things, keep her prisoner. Already, his magic affected her. She found it hard to think clearly. "Let me witness you letting the Shepherd and the two scouts go. Let go of my arm. I'm not a child."

He laughed. "Why so suspicious? My word is good." But he did release her arm.

"I want to see those men being freed. I want to see them walk away from here. Otherwise, I'm not doing anything."

"All right." He said something and two monks came forward with the Shepherd between them. His face was pale with red welts across his cheeks. From where he'd been hit?

He pleaded. "Don't, Johanna. Please, don't give in to him. Your life is worth more than mine."

Johanna stepped close to him and whispered in the space between his shoulder and neck, "Go to the river. You'll find a boat there. Wait for me on the other side. Save Roald." The Shepherd nodded, his eyes wide.

Johanna stepped back. "Let him go. I will stay and hear what you have to say."

She kept her back straight and rubbed her arm where he had touched her. The skin was still tingling.

She watched the Shepherd and the two young scouts walk into the night down the path. She hoped that Roald and Karl were smart enough to follow.

Then Kylian put his hand across her back on her hip. "Let's go inside, shall we?"

CHAPTER 20

FTER THE SHEPHERD had gone from sight, Kylian led her past the pond through the fields. Mist pooled in the valley turning the vineyards into ghostly shapes.

The monks accompanied them as silent sentinels. Johanna felt oddly calm inside. Somehow, ever since that dance at the palace, she had known that it would come to this meeting. Whatever attracted him to her, he needed to be disabused of the notion that she should come with him. She would calmly explain to him that she was committed to Saardam and Roald, and that it was neither shameful nor strange to love someone who wasn't normal.

They went up the lane that led to the house. From the field came the sound of honking geese.

One of the monks ran into the field waving a stick to chase them off.

"Those things are a menace," Kylian said, and it was the first thing he'd said since Shepherd Carolus had left.

"They're only geese," Johanna said. She thought of Roald's dislike for the birds, and hoped that Roald was crossing the river right now. Not sure. She could see parts of the silver ribbon of water between the trees.

Kylian lit a storm lamp at the steps.

They went into a wooden door which creaked badly and gave access to a barn full of shovels, picks, hoes, rakes, wheelbarrows and other equipment that cast long, tangled shadows by the light from the lamp. Against the far wall, there were a couple of long tables covered with tiny grapes. For making raisins, she guessed. Mice rustled in dark places where she could not see them.

From that large room they went to another, this one a well-appointed farm kitchen with a large stove, an open fire and pots and pans on neat shelves. The air was heavy with the smell of smoke and food. A monk was kneading dough at the table and another was cutting onions. He greeted Kylian with a bow of the head.

Johanna's stomach rumbled.

Kylian spoke briefly to both men and they responded with polite nods. A young boy came into the hall with them, carrying a candle.

Kylian took Johanna into a lush sitting room where the boy lit a few oil lamps. A lusty fire burned in the hearth. He gestured for Johanna to sit down on one of the couches and sat down on the other.

He said, "Dinner will be served shortly."

"This doesn't look much like a monastery."

"It used to be one. Abbot Guenther was an uncle of mine and after his death he bequeathed this building and the surrounding land to me."

"So it's no longer a religious place?"

"The land and the house are mine, but the monks are welcome to stay for as long as they want."

As long as they worked in his projects. "Do you still provide services for wayward royal sons?"

"Is that what you think we are? A work farm?"

"That's what it looks like from where I'm standing. That's what Roald has told me."

Kylian snorted.

She warned him, "Call him an idiot and my promise is off."

He let out a single huff of air that was a combination of a chuckle and a sigh. "Why so defensive of the idiot king?"

"He's my husband."

"A marriage of convenience, certainly."

"I happen to like him quite a lot."

"You can't be serious."

"No? Why is that such a surprise to you? He's smart, he knows a lot, and he's just awkward around people."

"I would have thought a smart girl like you could find someone better than that."

"You would like a smart girl like me to be hopelessly infatuated with you?"

He sniffed and let a silence lapse. From elsewhere in the building came sounds of voices. Then the door opened and a monk came in wheeling a trolley.

He pushed it to the table and set out two plates, glasses, knives and then a couple of bowls.

"The fare is quite simple here, but it's good," Kylian said.

When the monk had finished, they say down at the table. Kylian took his position opposite her.

The presence of the table between them made Johanna feel a little bit more relaxed. She let him pour her a drink from the carafe.

"Wine from the vineyard out there." He glanced at the window, where the last rays of daylight coloured the western sky.

The liquid was clear and sparkled in the glass. It smelled of grapes. Johanna took a small sip. "It's nice."

He sipped, too, and set his glass down. "Let me serve you."

He took her plate and carved a few slices off the roast leg of some sort of bird.

"Goose?" Johanna asked.

"You wish." He grinned.

And that set the tone for pleasant banter while they ate. Talking about food was safe, and she got the impression that he hadn't lied about being lonely.

She thought about his half-cousin Sylvan, who was often alone but never appeared to be lonely.

He had been right and the food was good. Johanna thought about Nellie, who would be out of her mind with worry right now, and maybe Loesie was behaving strangely again, and it worried her that Kylian was trying to keep her here, and that she must be strong against any magic he would try to use on her.

She prodded with her shoes for where the table legs were. Better not touch any wood here, considering the way he'd been trying to give her that splinter that would probably have told her about horrible things that had happened at the farm or in that hole in the ground.

After she finished her wine, he poured her another glass. The warmth from the hearth took the chill off the autumn air. The food was filling and the wine had made her sleepy.

"All right, enough now about the pleasant talk. Let's get to business. It's important that you know about this, because it affects all the known lands." He rose from the table, went to the desk and brought a roll of parchment, which, when he unrolled it, turned out to be a map.

Johanna blinked her eyes and squinted at it. Stupid. She shouldn't have had that second glass of wine. She was not used to it.

The map showed her the familiar outline of Saarland,

Burovia to the south all the way to the lands of the southern ocean where the coastline was drawn in rough, incomplete strokes and the map gave only names like *One Tree Island* scribbled in pen after the map was completed. Not places where people lived.

The land to the east of the Horn was left empty. No one knew how much land was there. In the ocean, the mapmaker had drawn a fanged, scaled creature with its mouth open, as if about to devour the ship that sailed there.

Kylian placed his index finger on that sea creature. "Danger is coming from this direction, and we must get ready to defend ourselves."

His voice sounded ominous, and he met her eyes squarely. He seemed to be quite sober, though he was swimming in and out of focus.

"How do you know that danger is coming?" she asked. Her tongue felt numb. Also, what did this danger have to do with the current situation in the low lands? If anything, the mess with Alexandre made the countries less able to defend themselves. "If you wanted to make us more defensible, wouldn't you want to unite all the countries, not wage war between them?"

"We need to use magic to defend ourselves," Kylian said. "These people who are coming are strong magicians."

Ah, now she understood. "And any church that prohibits magic is in the way, right? So you sent Alexandre?"

"We did not ask him to do what he did."

"But you were more than happy that he did it without your asking?"

"Many people have been unhappy about the influence of this church on our major sea port."

"So you killed the priests and burned the city."

"We rely on the cooperation of Saardam to supply us and

to protect us from the menace. Saardam will be in the front-line. They will come over the sea."

And he thought that attacking Saardam was the way to do that? "You are not listening to anything I say, aren't you?"

"No, you are not listening to anything I say. I've seen the danger on the wind. They have ships that need no wind. They have dragons. We need to act, or they will overrun us."

"If it's our cooperation you want, you have a strange way of going about it." She wished her head would stop swimming.

"If you would just allow me to give you this piece of wood, you would see it for yourself, and you would see that it is no trivial matter." He held the splinter out on his flat palm. How did that thing come here? She had dropped it and she hadn't seen him pick it up.

Johanna hesitated. She had been adamant that she would not touch any wood in this building. "I still can't see why you can't just tell me." She ignored his outstretched hand with the splinter.

"No words exist for some of the things that threaten us. They must be seen to be believed." He held his hand closer.

But the more he insisted that she touch the wood, the more she didn't want to do it. That splinter of wood held some sort of trickery, she was sure of that.

She made no move to pick it up, and he put it on the table between their plates. "You really don't trust me, right?"

"Having seen the evil magic you can perform, give me a reason why I should."

He pushed himself up from the table and walked around to her side. She thought he was going to sit next to her or touch her. In fact, he walked so close that the air that whirled in his wake brushed her face. Johanna did her best not to flinch.

He went to a cupboard behind her and took out a carafe

and two glasses. The fluid that sloshed against the glass was oily and bright green. *Absinthe*, the drink of demons and evil.

That was it.

"I think it is time for me to go." Johanna pushed herself up from her seat. Whoa, her head.

"Why the hurry?" He faced her.

A smile played across his lips. He said nothing, but that expression said enough. It said how he didn't think Roald was a worthy man for her. It said that for some reason he'd set his sights on her. It said that it was highly unlikely that she'd get out of this room with her dignity intact.

Johanna looked up into his face. Her heart was thudding. She saw his face as it had been on that first night in the palace, when he had danced with her, when he had kissed her.

"The people in the camp will be worried about me." Johanna's tongue wouldn't cooperate. Her cloak hung on a hook near the door.

"Such a pity," he said. "I'd have expected a bit more fire from you. But, alas. I'll walk you to the jetty." He retrieved her cloak from near the door.

All right, that was a lot easier than she had expected. Yet it didn't make sense. First he threatened to kill her or Roald, and now he was going to let her walk out of here, just like that?

"You seem disappointed," he said.

"That's not the word I'd use."

"But?"

"But what?"

"But you had expected me to be more insistent?" He trailed a finger over the skin in her neck. It gave her goose bumps.

"Something like that."

"I'm an honourable man." He held up the cloak and she

slipped into it. His close presence gave her the shivers. He smelled of horse and smoke.

"I appreciate a beautiful woman." He ran his hand over her hair, running the flyaway curls through his fingers. "But I know that she can't be mine, although I would beg on my knees for just one more kiss." His face hovered over hers.

"No," Johanna said. "My men are waiting for me."

He growled. "Your men are fools." He pulled her into the envelope of his smell and closed his mouth over hers. Johanna struggled. She tried to push him away, but he slid both his hands down her sides, holding her so tight against him that she could feel the heat of his body through his clothes. The magic burned in him. It sang to her, it pleaded with her—

No, he was just trying to trick her.

"Hmmm!" She pushed him away, but he was too strong. He forced her back until her back hit the wall. Nowhere to go. "Hmmmm!"

There was a sharp stabbing pain in her neck and the trickle of blood running down her skin. "Hmmm!"

Black spots danced in her vision. She saw giant flying creatures flapping huge leathery wings back lit by moonlight. She saw them open their mouths a spew fire. She saw a magician yell foreign words at them. His eyes were black as the night and his face glistened with sweat.

She was vaguely aware that Kylian picked her up with one arm under her shoulders and the other under her knees.

She saw ships coming into a foreign harbour. They were big and chunky, and the sails were red. Sea creatures reared from the water. Their big bodies coiled around her. Johanna tried to scream, but couldn't. The creature pulled her under water. She clawed at its scaled surface, trying to push herself free of its coils. She kicked, she scratched, she pummelled the scaled skin with both her fists. It held onto her neck with needle-sharp fangs buried deep into the flesh. The coils had pushed up her dress and a different part of the serpent held her in an entirely different way. It rubbed her in a pleasant way. It went inside her. It roared.

Glass shattered. A cold wind blasted through the room. Johanna fell and landed hard on her knees.

The lights were out and the fire had died. Blood trickled down her neck into her dress. She reached up. Her fingertips found the wooden splinter still buried in her skin. She pulled it out and stared at it by the light of the moon.

There was a sound nearby.

She wanted to whisper, "Who's there?" but her tongue was too dry. So she sat up and looked around her. Nothing. Where was Kylian? How long had she been out? Quite a while, she thought, judging by the stiffness of her muscles when she climbed to her feet. The floor was covered in grit, shards of porcelain and rubble. Her dress got caught under her feet, almost causing her to trip. The collar was wet from blood, but otherwise her clothing was intact. In the vision she had been *naked*. A shiver crawled over her back. The blood on her hands was starting to go sticky.

Footsteps in the corridor.

Johanna pressed herself against the wall.

Someone, no more than a ghostly shape, walked into the room. The glare of the moonlight showed only a light-coloured shirt. No one wore those, except . . .

"Roald?"

"Nobody touches my women," came Roald's voice out of the dark.

Johanna stumbled to the door. She didn't worry where Kylian was. Didn't care. She fell into Roald's arms. He'd been holding something—a broom or a shovel—which he dropped with a clang and held her awkwardly.

"You came back for me."

"I'm sorry we were late. We fell asleep. The Shepherd woke us up."

Magic. It was affecting them all. She should probably be angry that he hadn't obeyed her and hadn't left this side of the river, but for now, she was glad that he had come.

"I love you," she said into his chest.

"It's my task to say that."

She held him, feeling his warmth through the wetness of her clothes.

"We must get out of here quickly, Your Majesty." This voice belonged to Shepherd Carolus, whose presence was nothing more than a huge grey shape in the hall.

Johanna pushed herself out of Roald's arms. "Yes, we must go, immediately." Before Kylian turned up, wherever he had gone. Then she thought of the shovel Roald had been holding, and felt ill with the thought that Kylian might be lying on the floor unconscious somewhere in the house. Part of her wanted to go and look for him, to see if he was all right. That was the magic affecting her and she must fight it. She wouldn't ask Roald or Shepherd Carolus about him, or at least not until they were safely out of here. Not until there was no way magic could sabotage their escape.

Karl and the two scouts waited in the moonlit courtyard with Selmus the stallion. Roald lifted Johanna onto his warm and hairy back. There was no saddle. "I don't know if I can ride like this," She protested weakly. She was feeling dizzy all of a sudden.

"Hold on with your legs. We won't be going fast."

From somewhere within one of the surrounding buildings came a squawking. "What is that sound?"

"We locked the geese in the chapel," Karl said and he chuckled. "Someone will have a nasty surprise when he comes in for prayer tomorrow morning."

And by the lightening of the sky along the eastern horizon, the morning wasn't all that far away.

Roald took Selmus by the reins. Oh, those first few steps were wobbly. Johanna was still feeling dizzy and there was nowhere to hold on except the mane, but didn't everyone always say never hold on to a horse's mane? But after a while she became used to the horse's movement. Selmus was clearly a workhorse having endured much worse treatment than someone clumsily trying to stay on his back.

They left the courtyard for the main road that ran from the jetty to the hilltop farmhouse. The road sloped into a shallow valley where milking cows stood looking forlorn in the pre-dawn mist that hung low over the grass.

As they passed, swirls of mist oozed from the creek, stretching long ethereal fingers towards the road.

Shepherd Carolus at the front of the column hesitated. Roald stopped behind him, holding the horse's headgear.

"What is that mist doing?" the Shepherd said.

"Yeah, I don't like this one bit," said one of the scouts. Johanna believed the man's name was Willem. "See how the cows have all gotten up and come to the fence?"

They stood in a row facing the road.

"I've seen this happen at the chapel, but never here," the other man said.

"We didn't go this way often," Willem said.

"True."

"Keep going," Johanna said, her voice low. "Ignore it."

"The queen knows all about magic," the Shepherd said, and that scared Johanna more than anything. She knew nothing, except one thing: trying to get out of here was infinitely better than staying.

Slowly, they continued along the low-lying section of the road. The excess of rain had made the path muddy, but this area was naturally wet. Reeds and watercress grew in the meadows on either side.

Karl walked so close to the horse that Johanna's leg brushed his arm.

The mist continued branching out towards the road, now covering half the meadow. It was clear that they weren't going to make it to the jetty without having to confront whatever apparition was going to come out of the mist.

"Go and cut me a willow branch," Johanna said to Karl.

"But . . ." he said in a squeak.

"That tree over there." Johanna pointed.

He trotted to the fence and came back not much later with a long and floppy branch. What sort of willow was this?

Johanna held the twig, which resembled a whip more than a weapon.

And still the mist oozed out of the hollows and marshy areas. This entire land bled magic. Every person who ever died on this land had a ghost in that mist somewhere, because who ever died with all their business taken care of?

Their voices whispered in Johanna's ears. It didn't look like Roald of Karl could hear them, but they could definitely see the tendrils of mist that formed into human shapes, that crossed the meadow in the direction of the road, that reached emaciated, bony hands to the living humans. Many of them were apparitions, not senseless ghosts.

"Can we please go faster?" Karl's voice sounded high.

Roald urged the horse on. Whoa! That suddenly made the rocking worse. The horse's back was slippery with the animal's fine coat. Johanna squeezed her legs. She groped for the horse's mane. Never mind the horse wouldn't like it. Both Karl and Roald were almost running now. It was still a fair way to the jetty, and Johanna wasn't sure that she would be able to stay on. Her backside bumped onto the horse's back with each step it took.

"Wait, wait. Please stop. Let me down, I can walk—"

The road trembled. The gravel moved as if pushed up from underneath by a giant hand. A mount of dirt grew higher and higher until the top bloomed open. A hiss of cold air streamed out. Karl screamed. The horse reared. Johanna slid from its back into the mud.

Ouch. She sat in the wet grass while water seeped up her skirt. The two scouts were running to the jetty. Roald had grabbed Selmus' reins and was trying to calm the horse, but the white showed in the corners of the horse's eyes. Shepherd Carolus stood in the middle of the road chanting prayers. He held up his pendant with the sign of the Triune.

Where was the willow branch? She crawled on her hands and knees in the mud, her movements restricted by her wet clothes.

"Look, look!" Karl yelled.

Johanna didn't need to look to know that a ghost had emerged. The man's figure was brilliant white with flowing, curly hair. His face had strong cheekbones and intense, not too deep-set eyes. His chin was strong but not angular. His nose was straight without being sharp or thin. His lips were full. It was the most handsome man she had ever seen. It was a perfect version of Kylian.

What? "What did you do to him with that shovel?" she asked Roald.

"The idiot did nothing," Kylian said and laughed. "He couldn't harm me if he tried. I am one of the few people who can transcend the borders between life and death at will."

No one could do that. It was a trick. It had to be.

"Keep away from her," Roald said, lifting the shovel. Johanna realised *It has a wooden handle*.

"Give that to me." She pulled at it.

"I will protect you."

"You can't protect me from magic and keep control of the

horse at the same time. Take the horse and the others to safety." She managed to get hold of the handle—she saw a monk shovelling manure from the barn into a cart—and faced the apparition.

The men stared at her.

"No, Johanna!" Roald called.

Johanna shouted, "Run to the boat! Now. Go!"

They backed away, hesitantly.

The apparition said. "You have worked it out. We can be dispelled with a simple piece of wood. But that doesn't even come close to killing us. Nothing can kill us. We always come back bigger and more frightening." He reached out, and Johanna held the shovel before her.

He laughed, but backed away from the wood. "Run now, little princess. You will live a bit longer. There will be a day that you will come back to beg me for my help. That day may be sooner than you think."

His ghostly form dissolved. Ice-cold wind whooshed over her head.

CHAPTER 21

JOHANNA RAN.

Roald and Karl were already in the dinghy with the Shepherd and the two scouts still on the jetty. Roald was trying to reel in the sea cows' ropes, but the animals were nervous and kept tangling the gear. They clambered in the boat, which wobbled with the weight of all these people. Karl kept a nervous eye on the water level on the outside of the hull.

The sea cows were tugging at the harness. It was impossible to reel them in so they'd have to do that after casting off. Johanna unhooked the rope from the pylon and the animals took off with such speed that she almost fell overboard. They tore across the churning expanse of water.

A dense mist hung over the far bank, blanketing the camp. Even before the forms of the tents resolved from the mist, the sound of shouts drifted in the stillness.

A chill went over Johanna's back. "Did anything happen in the camp?"

No one knew the answer to that question.

Johanna peered through the mist.

People were running down the riverbank and up the jetty, men women and children, all bunching into a large group in front of the *Prosperity*'s gangplank.

A man yelled. "Oh, look, they're back!"

"They've got the Shepherd!"

"And Ko and Willem."

"Thank the heavens."

It looked like half the camp was there, and a lot of people carried bags, too.

Johanna tossed the rope up the jetty and climbed out of the boat. Many hands helped the men up. The young scouts both had family in the camp who greeted them with squeals of happiness. The Shepherd received a hero's welcome.

A man yelled, "Make room for the king and queen!"

People shuffled aside to form a path.

Johanna spotted Captain Arense. "What's going on?"

"The camp was overrun by ghosts this morning," he said. "They came out of the river and all the marsh areas and drifted between the tents. Some people tried to fight them with burning torches, and some tents caught fire. Some are still burning."

"Was anyone hurt?"

"Not badly, no. People panicked and came here. We decided that we're leaving. I don't know what we'll find downstream, but it can't be any worse than this."

Johanna nodded. She agreed.

There were a lot of people already crammed on board the *Prosperity* and more people continued to climb aboard. Her eyes met those of Johan Delacoeur across the crowd. He didn't sneer. In fact, his expression was haunted. It had taken a long time, but Johanna thought he finally believed her. He gave a barely perceptible nod. She nodded back at him. A tiny measure of respect.

There was a great splashing in the water, where a sea cow

threshed its tail on the surface while the deck hand tried to reel in the ropes. The animals were nervous, too. They wouldn't come. They wormed themselves out of their harnesses. They tangled up the ropes.

Loesie and Nellie stood with Master Deim in the deck of the *Lady Sara*

"Get the animals!" Johanna called out to Loesie and Loesie ran to the front, hopefully to do as ordered.

On the other side of the jetty, Karl was leading people to the *Prosperity*. Men in the camp were still trying to put out the fires which burned in the hay stores and some of the primitive wooden constructions that served as outdoor kitchen or overflow housing. There was no sign of any ghosts, but the sun was rising and ghosts did not usually appear in sunlight. Who knew what the night would bring, though? They were downstream from the farm, and the murky, magic-infused water flowed right past the camp. She had always wondered why the Baron hadn't offered a field closer to town. Now she knew.

Captain Arense yelled that everyone should go down into the hold. Wives called for husbands or children. It was too dark down in the hold to recognise faces.

She called, "Anyone who can't find a spot, come to the *Lady Sara*."

A line of people started up the gangplank to the *Lady Sara*. Nellie guided them to the rear deck and to begin filling up the hold covers from the rear. Entire families dumped their bags, blankets and other meagre possessions onto the lids. Johanna hoped that there was going to be enough room for everyone. The part of the camp she could see was starting to look deserted. Some people had even taken down the tents and covered themselves and others with the canvas. Roald had taken care of a couple of young children. One of the girls carried a lamb.

She shouted to Captain Arense, "Do you think we have everyone?"

Everyone who wanted to come, at any rate. She hadn't seen either Ignatius Hemeldinck or Fleuris LaFontaine.

Whether the camp was empty or not, they were out of time. A couple of the Baron's men rode into the camp from the main road. Their horses moved in full gallop, manes and hair flying. The first one carried a banner.

Johanna panicked. *Kylian.*

People on the deck had seen them, too, and panicked talk spread over the deck.

"Get ready, we're out of here!" Johanna yelled at Loesie and Nellie.

She cast the first rope loose. Then she ran to the back deck and loosened the second one. The rope was rough and cut her hands when sliding around the post. While the horses came down the riverbank, the *Lady Sara* drifted away from the jetty. The horses tore over the wooden planks with a thundering of hooves. Johanna held her breath. The front rider rode a warhorse and carried a sword and crossbow. He wasn't going to jump, was he?

The gap between the jetty and the boat grew, but not fast enough for her liking.

Johanna bit her lip. *Come on, come on, come on.*

The horse came closer and closer—

And the rider pulled hard on the reins. The horse slid to a halt and reared with a screaming neigh. His comrades pulled up behind with a good amount of snorting and swearing.

The *Lady Sara* and *Prosperity* drifted away from the shore, with nothing but churning, magic-infused water separating them.

The leader yelled across the water. Obscenities, no doubt.

The current pulled hard at the ship. Loesie and Roald had

managed to pull in the sea cows in their proper formation and gave them free rein to swim as fast as they could.

Behind them, a man's voice yelled, "Eeeeyup!" and there was the sharp sound of a stick being banged against the hull to frighten the animals into going faster. Johanna spotted Master Deim and Karl on the deck.

The Baron's men turned their horses away from the jetty and ran along the river bank, but slowed down in the marshy area of tangled branches where, just days ago, she and Master Deim had found Loesie. The horses found no easy path through this area, and they were left further and further behind.

The sounds of their angry yelling faded until the only thing left was the sound of sloshing water against the hull. The sun was just coming up over the misty landscape, edging the world in gold.

"We're going home," a man said behind her, in an incredulous voice.

"Yes, we're going home!" another shouted.

"Long live the King! Long live the Queen!"

Roald had been sitting on the hold covers with the young children he had helped. The girl had handed him her lamb, which he held cradled in his lap. Johanna went to pull him up, and he rose, still holding the animal.

"You're going to have to behave in a kingly way," she said to him.

"No. That's why I have you." He put an arm around her waist.

So they stood amongst their citizens: a painfully shy and awkward king who liked frogs and ducklings, an inexperienced queen and a lamb that symbolised the child they desperately needed but that had still not shown any sign of appearing.

At least they were going home.

A Word of Thanks

THANK YOU very much for reading the Idiot King. The story is not finished here! In the next book, *Fire Wizard*, the refugees return to Saardam and learn of the real reason for the occupation of Saardam.

As author of this book, I would appreciate it very much if you could return to the place where you purchased this book and leave a review. Reviews are important to me, because they help readers decide if the book is for them.

ABOUT THE AUTHOR

Patty Jansen lives in Sydney, Australia, where she spends most of her time writing Science Fiction and Fantasy.

Her story *This Peaceful State of War* placed first in the second quarter of the Writers of the Future contest and was published in their 27th anthology. She has also sold fiction to genre magazines such as Analog Science Fiction and Fact, Redstone SF and Aurealis.

Patty has written over twenty novels in both Science Fiction and Fantasy, including the *Icefire Trilogy* and the *Ambassador* series.

pattyjansen.com

BOOKS BY PATTY JANSEN

More information:

PATTYJANSEN.COM